The group in the living room fell silent and strained their ears.

Kurt was right. There was a sound, like a chain saw or an airplane, coming from outside.

"It's the National Guard," Sam quipped, "dropping us supplies by parachute. Please, I need junk food!"

"Quiet!" Kurt said.

The sound got louder and louder, until it was almost deafening—it clearly was an airplane, probably a small one. And judging from the sporadic sputtering of the engine, this was an airplane in trouble.

"Come on!" Kurt shouted. He ran outside and everyone tumbled after him.

And there, from the front porch of the house, Emma, Sam, and Carrie saw something they would never forget for the rest of their lives.

In the bright light of the full moon, they watched as a small single-engine airplane seemed to stop in midair, and then slowly, ever so slowly, plummet to the ground.

The SUNSET ISLAND series
by Cherie Bennett

Sunset Island
Sunset Kiss
Sunset Dreams
Sunset Farewell
Sunset Reunion
Sunset Secrets
Sunset Heat
Sunset Promises
Sunset Scandal
Sunset Whispers
Sunset Paradise
Sunset Surf
Sunset Deceptions
Sunset on the Road
Sunset Embrace
Sunset Wishes

Sunset Touch
Sunset Wedding
Sunset Glitter
Sunset Stranger
Sunset Heart
Sunset Revenge
Sunset Sensation
Sunset Magic
Sunset Illusions
Sunset Fire
Sunset Fantasy
Sunset Passion
Sunset Love
Sunset Fling
Sunset Tears
Sunset Spirit

The CLUB SUNSET ISLAND series
by Cherie Bennett

Too Many Boys!
Dixie's First Kiss
Tori's Crush

Also created by Cherie Bennett

Sunset After Dark
Sunset After Midnight
Sunset After Hours

Sunset Holiday

CHERIE BENNETT

Sunset™
Island

SPLASH™

A BERKLEY / SPLASH BOOK

SUNSET HOLIDAY is an original publication of
The Berkley Publishing Group.
This work has never appeared before in book form.

SUNSET HOLIDAY

A Berkley Book / published by arrangement with
General Licensing Company, Inc.

PRINTING HISTORY
Berkley edition / November 1995

A GLC BOOK

Splash and *Sunset Island* are trademarks belonging to
General Licensing Company, Inc.

ISBN: 0-425-15109-3

BERKLEY®
Berkley Books are published by
The Berkley Publishing Group,
200 Madison Avenue, New York, New York 10016.
BERKLEY and the "B" design
are trademarks belonging to Berkley Publishing Corporation.

PRINTED IN THE UNITED STATES OF AMERICA

10 9 8 7 6 5 4 3 2 1

For the big guy who
keeps me warm in the winter

Sunset
Holiday

ONE

"Pres, I'm freezing," Samantha Bridges said, a shiver running through her.

"It's ninety-five degrees in the sun," her boyfriend, Presley Travis, said, turning over onto his back. He settled his head back down on the old beach blanket the two of them had brought to the beach that afternoon. "Gotta watch the time," he murmured. "I have to be back at work in twenty minutes."

"I'm really freezing," Sam said, her teeth beginning to chatter.

He opened his eyes and peered at her. "You sick, sweet thang?" he asked in his sexy Southern drawl.

"I don't know," Sam replied. "It's weird. My hand is so cold. . . ."

Pres sat up and gathered Sam into his arms. "If that's just an excuse to get me to hug you, it's working," he said with a grin. "Better?"

Sam nodded. "But my hand . . . it's still freezing," she managed to gasp out.

"We could bury it in the sand," Pres suggested, reaching for her hand. "Or I could stick that puppy in my armpit—"

"That's disgusting!" Sam said with a laugh.

"Or I could kiss you until you forget you even have a hand," Pres said, leaning closer.

"My hand is *still* freezing," Sam complained, shaking her wild red curls out of her eyes. "I mean it, it's—"

She woke up with a start.

"Wha . . . ?" she said, looking around the brightly lit room, dazed.

Her two best friends, Emma Cresswell and Carrie Alden, sat together on the floor just to the side of the bed. They were both giggling and pointing to Sam's right hand.

It was lying on top of a bucket of snow the two of them had brought into the huge log cabin.

"Jeez," Sam said. "Great timing. I was having the most fantastic dream, and you two went and ruined it."

"I bet," Carrie said with a laugh. "You were puckering your lips in your sleep."

"Pres," Emma said with a sigh.

"Of course," Carrie agreed with a smile.

Sam lay back on the bed and stared dreamily at the ceiling. "We were at the beach, the sun was beating down on us—"

"Sounds nice," Emma said wistfully.

"What time is it?" Sam asked, sitting up in bed.

"Noon," Carrie reported.

"You're kidding," Sam said, getting out of bed and walking over to the window. Bright sunlight reflected off the deep snow. "No, I guess you're not," she corrected herself.

3

"You slept forever," Emma said, stretching. "We figured the snow would wake you up."

"You want breakfast?" Carrie asked.

"Let me get dressed," Sam said sleepily. "I'll be right out."

"Let us know if you want some more snow," Emma said playfully as she and Carrie left the room.

As Sam quickly showered and pulled on some old jeans and a Disney World sweatshirt (from the brief time she'd worked there as a dancer), she thought back on the amazing circumstances that not only had made her best friends with Carrie and Emma, but now had brought the three of them together again for a winter reunion in Vermont.

All three girls had met at the International Au Pair Convention in New York City. They'd each decided to seek summer work as au pairs, and they'd come to the convention to try to find jobs. They'd quickly become friends.

Luck had been on their side. All of them got hired by families that summered on spectacular Sunset Island, the world-famous resort island off the coast of Maine at the far end of Casco Bay, not too distant from the city of Portland. They'd now spent two summers together there.

It's amazing that we're best friends, Sam mused as she brushed out her long, wild red hair in the tiny mirror over the dresser, *because we're all so different from each other. We even look totally different!*

Emma is a Boston heiress, and her family has more money than I'll ever see in my lifetime—though her mother recently cut her off from her money because she doesn't like Emma's boyfriend. She has perfect blond hair, perfect looks, a perfect petite body, perfect everything.

Carrie, meanwhile, comes from New Jersey, where her parents are both doctors. She's got, like, a straight-A average at Yale. And hooters! Something I don't have, Sam thought ruefully. *She also is the most level-headed person I know. Yeah, she thinks she looks like the girl next door and is a little too curvy, but I think she looks great. And she'd look even better if she wore some makeup.*

And then there's me, Sam ruminated, absentmindedly working out a tangle in her hair with the brush. *I'm good at dancing. And designing clothes. And I'll try anything once. But I dropped out of college, and I found out just this year—at the age of nineteen—that I'm adopted, and . . . I'm still a virgin. That's one thing Emma and I have in common.*

Sam stretched out to her full five feet ten inches, pulled her hair back in a ponytail, and shrugged at herself.

That'll change, Sam thought as she closed the door to her room and went to join her friends in the kitchen. *Eventually. But I'm not doing anything until I'm ready—whenever that is.*

"I can't get over how amazing this place is," Sam said as she breezed into the kitchen toward the smell of freshly brewed coffee. Emma and Carrie were sitting at the kitchen table, nibbling on some peanut butter cookies they'd baked the day before.

"It's great to have a rich aunt," Carrie joshed.

Emma blushed. "She's a great person." *And I think she likes me more than my own mother does,* Emma added in her mind. *At least Aunt Liz hasn't ever disinherited me!*

"It was really nice of her to let us use this place," Carrie said, sipping her coffee.

"She's terrific," Emma agreed, pouring herself a cup of coffee.

"You're drinking coffee?" Sam asked. "I thought you only drank tea."

"It smells so good, I thought I'd try it," Emma said, taking a sip. She made a face. "Why is it that coffee always smells better than it tastes?"

"I love the way it tastes," Sam said, adding two heaping spoonfuls of sugar to her cup. She poured in some cream and took a loud slurp. "Yum," she said, looking around happily. "You know, this place is like a palace."

Sam was right. Emma's Aunt Liz—her mother's sister—had allowed Emma and her friends to use her Vermont vacation house over the Christmas holidays while she was traveling in Asia as part of her work for the Environmental Defense Fund. And what a house it was!

The place was a gigantic log cabin, built on a hillside overlooking a lake. There were three bedrooms, a huge kitchen, an enormous living room with a wood-burning fireplace in the center, and three full bathrooms. Upstairs was a small sleeping loft. And to top it all off, out back was a beautiful hot tub big enough to hold eight people in its steamy, bubbling water.

That's good, Sam thought quickly, *because the high temperature yesterday didn't get much above ten degrees!*

"I think it's incredible we could all get together here for Christmas," Carrie marveled, taking a bite of a third cookie. She stared at the cookie, then put it down on the table. *Just because I'm on vacation doesn't mean I can pig out*, she told herself.

"Thank Aunt Liz," Emma said.

"I'm thanking her," Sam quipped, taking a handful of cookies from the plate.

Actually, Sam thought, *it is pretty in-credible how this all came about. Emma called me a couple of weeks ago and said that her aunt Liz had this vacation house in northern Vermont that was going to be empty over the holidays. Like I really had the money to go to Vermont.*

But then Billy called me a couple of days afterward to say that the Flirts had gotten a gig at a concert hall in Burling-ton, not too far from Emma's aunt's house, for a few days before Christmas. And that Polimar Records was going to pay to bring us in to perform!

And now we're all here.

"You know," Sam said, popping an-other cookie into her mouth, "this is all too incredible. I mean, how it's worked out and everything. Don't you think?"

"It is amazing," Carrie agreed, wiping her mouth with a napkin. "That we're all here. Even Erin!"

The Flirts' gig had turned out to be an occasion for a Sunset Island reunion. Of course, all the guys in the band were there: Billy Sampson, who was Carrie's

9

boyfriend; Presley Travis; Jay Bailey, the mild-mannered piano player they sometimes called "Wild Man"; and Jake Fisher, the cute new drummer. Emma, Sam, and Erin Kane had gone along to sing backup; Kurt Ackerman, Emma's boyfriend, had agreed to serve as road manager; and Billy had asked Carrie to take some photos of the gig.

Recently the Flirts' original drummer, Sly Smith, had died of AIDS. Sam shuddered and felt a lump in her throat. *I still can't believe it,* she thought, *even though I was at his funeral.* She gulped hard and tried to throw off her sad thought by changing the subject. "Hey, do you think things between Erin and Jake are heating up?"

Emma shrugged. "Ask Erin."

"I'd rather speculate and come to my own wild conclusions," Sam said, wiggling her eyebrows.

Erin Kane was the backup singer who had replaced their archenemy, Diana De-Witt, when she'd been thrown out of the band. Erin was a fantastic singer and a really great girl. She had long, curly blond hair and a beautiful face. She was also at least fifty pounds overweight. Somehow she pulled it off and looked great. She and Jake had been dating for a while now.

"We're not all here," Sam groused.

"Who's missing?" Carrie asked.

"Just my two favorite people in the whole world," Sam said, her voice completely deadpan.

"Who's that?" Emma queried. "Becky and Allie Jacobs?"

"Good guess," Sam replied. "But wrong."

All three girls laughed. Becky and Allie were the twin fourteen-year-olds Sam took care of when she was on Sunset Island. The twins were extremely precocious and had really big mouths. Sam like to call them "the monsters," and they often deserved the nickname.

"Okay," Carrie said, setting her coffee cup down on the table, "I've got it."

"The two-headed she-devil from hell," they all said together, laughing.

The two-headed she-devil consisted of

Diana De Witt and Lorell Courtland, two girls who summered on Sunset Island and seemed to have no purpose in life other than to make the three friends' lives miserable.

"Can you believe Diana actually used to sing with us?" Sam recalled.

"I loathe her," Emma said.

Not only do I loathe her, Emma added in her mind, *but she practically ruined my relationship with Kurt, when he actually slept with her after the two of us came close to breaking up* . . .

"I loathe her more," Sam said, reaching for another cookie. "God help me if I ever have to sing next to her again."

"Hey," Carrie said, getting up from the table, "want to go see how the guys are doing?"

"Where are they, anyway?" Sam asked.

"Ice fishing," Emma said. She got up from the table, too, and carried her coffee cup to the dishwasher.

"*Ice fishing*?" Sam repeated. "You're asking me if I want to go watch them *ice fishing*?"

"Why not?" Carrie asked.

"Because it involves ice," Sam replied, downing the last of her coffee. "And it involves fishing."

"So your answer is no," Carrie said, starting to gather the other dirty dishes off the table.

"Correct-amundo," Sam said. "You guys can give me the full report. I'm hitting the hot tub in the back."

"Erin's out there on the ice," Carrie said.

"Erin has more padding than I do," Sam joked.

Neither Carrie nor Emma laughed.

"Well, it's true!" Sam cried defensively. Then she felt guilty. "Bad joke, huh?" she said meekly.

Emma smiled at her. "You're actually developing a conscience, Sam!"

"Yeah, well, " Sam said. "Don't let it get around. My rep will be ruined."

"Come on out on the lake with us," Carrie urged her. "It'll be fun."

"Right," Sam said. "It's my idea of a good time, all right."

"What's that?" Carrie asked, sounding puzzled.

"Frostbite," Sam answered. "A terminal case of frostbite."

"There they are!" Carrie cried as the three neared the frozen lake. She pointed to a small knot of people about a hundred yards away.

"They look like they're having fun," Emma said, hearing some laughter from the group of their friends.

That's Kurt, laughing the loudest, Emma thought happily. *I love the sound of his laugh. In fact, I love everything about him. I'm so glad he was able to come on this reunion with us! I know how tight his budget is, and I know what a sacrifice it is.*

"Their minds have been frozen," Sam quipped. She pulled her red scarf more tightly around her ears. "When do we go back? It's freezing."

"It's not even that cold today," Emma said as they continued walking toward their friends.

"I beg to differ," Sam retorted, the thin layer of snow on the lake crunching under her boots. "You're from Boston. You're used to this!"

"Catch anything?" Carrie called to the others.

Billy Sampson picked something off the ice and held it up, a big smile on his face.

"Lake trout!" Pres yelled out.

"It's huge!" Emma called.

"Four-pounder," said Kurt with excitement.

"Look!" Sam called. "What's that?" Out of the corner of her eye, she'd seen a flag go up at one of the five or six fishing devices her friends had made, that were scattered across their area of the lake.

"Fish!" Jay Bailey exclaimed. Everyone went running over to the ice-fishing tip-up, and Sam was surprised to find that she too was excited to see what they'd caught. *Well, it'll be dinner, after all*, she told herself.

They crowded in a circle around the hole in the ice as Kurt flipped his gloves off, picked up the tip-up, and quickly and expertly began pulling in the line.

"Big one," Kurt breathed. "I can feel it."

Kurt battled the fish for a couple of minutes, actually having to give back some line a couple of times as the fish made a run under the ice. Finally he had the fish close to the surface.

"Whoa, baby," Sam said as Kurt pulled the fish's head up through the hole in the ice, grabbed it with his other hand, and then neatly flipped the nearly three-foot-long, skinny fish onto the ice, where it proceeded to thrash around wildly.

"What is it?" Erin asked.

"Pickerel," Kurt said knowledgeably. "Check out those teeth."

"Looks like Diana," Sam remarked as she peered into the fish's mouth, which featured two rows of razor-sharp teeth. She made a face. "Excuse me, but this is seriously gross."

"Fishing?" Erin asked with surprise.

"How can this be a sport?" Sam went on. "I mean, fish are stupid, right? They're down there, swimming around, like la-de-da, and then you come along with a free lunch on a hook. Give me a break!"

"Does the hook hurt them?" Emma asked tentatively.

"Not really," Billy said. "Honest."

"Okay, who's gonna kiss this fish?" Jake asked. "For a buck."

"A buck?" Sam echoed. "Please! We're talking a Diana-fish here. Kindly up the stakes!"

"Okay, five bucks," Jake said with a laugh.

"I'm your girl," Sam said, stepping forward in a show of bravado.

"Such bravery!" Carrie teased.

"Hey, I kiss Pres," Sam quipped. "What's the difference?"

"Keep your nose out of Diana's way, sweetheart," Pres advised. "Its teeth are sharp."

"Aw, you think that fish is gonna bite me?" Sam taunted. She reached over and picked it up with both hands.

"Careful," Emma cautioned.

Sam made a move as if she was going to kiss the pickerel on the nose, then quickly put it back down on the ice and blew it a big kiss.

"Hey, no fair," Erin quipped.

"I only pay for a direct smack on the lips," Jake said.

"Fish don't have lips," Emma said with a laugh. "Do they?"

"No, but I do," Kurt told her, and leaned over and kissed her softly.

"Awwww," the group teased.

It feels like home, Sam thought as she glanced around the circle of friends. *I've missed these guys so much. Nothing could possibly go wrong to spoil this reunion. We've all been through so much lately— Billy's leukemia scare and his dad's accident, Emma's mother disinheriting her, and the worst of all, Sly's death. We all just need some time to be together with no big crises to get in the way.*

Just a wonderful, relaxing holiday.

She hoped.

TWO

"So let me go over it again," Billy Sampson said with the rest of the gang gathered around him in Aunt Liz's gorgeous living room. He and Carrie were sitting on the plush couch, directly facing the fireplace.

"We got it, O fearless leader," Sam said, shifting her feet in the direction of the blazing fire. "Road trip to the club the day after tomorrow, departure two-thirty sharp."

"That's right," Billy agreed. "We'll do a quick rehearsal and sound check, and then the show is at eight."

"Who's coming from Polimar?" Emma asked.

19

Billy shook his head. "Don't know. Maybe Shelly Plotkin, maybe the other guy." Shelly Plotkin was the Polimar A&R executive who'd first become interested in the band. But when it came time actually to sign them, a very businesslike guy named Cody Leete had made the trek to their gig in Maine.

It was later that evening. The guys had cooked the fish they had caught, and the girls had made a giant salad and baked potatoes to go with it. Now, an hour after dinner, everyone was sprawled around the living room, digesting their food and just relaxing. Erin and Jake had been playing chess when Billy started talking about the gig.

"What if the weather gets bad?" Erin asked. "What do we do then?"

"How bad is bad?" Sam asked.

"Bad as in we get snowed in," Erin said.

"Basically, we're completely screwed," Billy said cheerfully.

"Dog team," Sam cracked. "We go by dog team."

"Woof, woof," Jay Bailey joked.

"It's a good forecast," Pres drawled. "So far, anyway."

Sam and her friends nodded. They'd all watched the news together right before dinner. And while snow was forecast for later in the week, the next couple of days were supposed to be sunny. Cold, but sunny.

"This should be fun," Emma said softly. Her head was resting in Kurt's lap, and he was gently stroking her hair.

"I'm looking forward to playing for our good friends at Polimar again, man," Billy said. His tone was sarcastic.

"Chill, bro," Pres cautioned him.

"It sucks, man," Billy went on, his voice getting more upset. "They sign us to a deal, and then . . ." He shook his head in frustration.

Sam looked down at the floor. She knew exactly what Billy was getting so upset about, since he'd been sending everyone in the band periodic updates over the last few months.

The good news was that Polimar

Records, which had courted Flirting With Danger for two entire summers, finally had signed the band to a record deal.

And the bad news is that once they signed us, they hardly did anything for us, Sam recalled. *Lots of promises about CDs and videos, but nothing much has really happened.*

"They're springing for this gig," Jake reminded Billy.

"Yeah," Billy said. "Big wow."

"We'll just have to kick butt the night after next," Pres said, his voice mild.

Billy looked at the others. "Sorry, guys," he said, an abashed smile on his face. "It's just getting to me a little. The last time I tried to call Polimar about our CD, they put me on hold four times—and I still never got a straight answer out of them."

"Don't worry about it, man," Pres said.

"You think people are actually going to come to a show just a few days before Christmas?" Kurt asked skeptically.

"We'll see, won't we?" Billy mused.

Carrie, who was sitting next to him,

reached for his hand. *He's really worried,* she thought. *I can tell.*

"Well, it could be worse," Sam said, sitting up and brightening.

"How?" Billy challenged her. "What can be worse than being signed to a deal and then having the record company ignore you?"

"Flash Hathaway could be their official photographer," Sam said, her face deadpan.

Everyone cracked up, and some of the tension in the room melted away.

"Flash Hathaway," Billy said, grinning. "I haven't thought of him in a long time."

"I bet he hasn't thought of you, either," Carrie joked, leaning against Billy. *This feels so right,* she thought with contentment. *As if he and I are meant to sit by each other forever and ever.*

"What a wanker," Kurt said, shaking his head.

You can say that again, Sam reflected, thinking back two summers. *I can't believe that the guy got me to pose practi-*

cally naked for him, and then displayed the photographs in a private club! If it hadn't been for Jane Hewitt's great legal advice, I would have been totally humiliated.

"There was one great thing, though," Billy recalled as he put his arm around Carrie.

"What's that?" Kurt asked.

"When Johnny Angel totally trashed Flash's camera equipment at Madison Square Garden!" Billy chortled. He laughed at the memory, and his remaining anger about Polimar seemed to fade away.

Everyone laughed, including Sam.

God, was I dumb then, she thought. *I can't believe I was actually flirting with Johnny Angel. And Flash took a picture of the two of us together, and got it printed in some New York tabloid!*

Sam sneaked a glance at Pres. He winked at her.

He knows what I'm thinking about, she thought. *He totally knows.*

Sam looked at Emma and Carrie. "Guess who's my other favorite character out of our Sunset Island past," she ordered.

"Dan Jacobs?" Carrie ventured, mentioning the name of Sam's boss, the twins' father.

"Nope."

"X?" Emma asked.

"Buff," Sam answered, remembering the gay dancer's amazing physique, "but no cigar."

"Hey, how come we're not in this game?" Pres drawled.

"Girl talk," Sam said matter-of-factly.

"I know," Carrie said. "Butchie Gleason!"

"Bingo!" Sam cried. "Remember the time when you played pool at the Play Café against him?"

"You beat him," Emma reminded Carrie.

"Correction," Sam said. "You busted his butt."

"And he still calls you 'Big Red,'" Carrie said.

"Yeah," Sam said. "I don't know who I miss more, Butchie Gleason or Flash."

"I'll tell you who I miss," Billy said, standing up for a moment and stretching. "Sly."

No one spoke for a few moments as they each remembered their friend and bandmate in their own way. Finally it was Emma who broke the silence.

"I feel like he's here," she said simply, her voice soft.

"He'd want to be here," Pres agreed. "He'd be all ticked off about something— you know how prickly he could get."

"He'd say we weren't practicing enough," Billy agreed fondly.

"He *is* here," Carrie said. "In our memories."

And then everyone was quiet again.

Erin stood up. "I think I might be getting a sore throat," she said quietly. "I'd better go to bed."

Sam looked up at the ceiling. "Sly," she said, "you'd better not let Erin get sick!"

Everyone laughed. Then, Sam felt Emma take her hand, and she took Jay's, who was sitting next to her. And around the room, everyone held hands with everyone else.

They were all together, but one part was missing: Sly Smith. Sam knew, though, that they would never, ever allow themselves to forget.

"Liz Barrington's home, Emma Cresswell speaking," Emma said as she picked up the phone in the living room, where she, Carrie and Sam were catching up with each other.

"May we speak with Sam Bridges?" two voices said at the same time. They both had British accents. Emma didn't recognize the voices, and she was surprised that someone would be calling her Aunt Liz's house to try to find Sam.

It was an hour or so later that same evening. Erin had already gone off to bed, and Billy and the guys had decided to go for a walk in the moonlight on the frozen lake. Which left Sam, Carrie, and Emma together in the living room, to talk and catch up with each other.

"Sam," Emma said, holding her hand over the mouthpiece, "it's for you."

"Tell 'em to go away," Sam ordered. "I'm too comfortable." She stretched out languorously on the rug in front of the fireplace.

"Sam," Emma repeated, holding out the receiver.

"Who is it?" Sam asked. "Butchie Gleason?"

The girls all laughed. Emma put the phone back up by her ear.

"Who may I tell her is calling?" she asked in her usual patrician tones.

"You dare ask?" one of the voices asked. Her British accent was thick and clipped.

"Yes, I dare," Emma said, surprised.

"Well, I never!" the voice said, clearly offended.

Emma put her hand over the phone again. "This very bizarre woman on the phone doesn't want to identify herself," she told Sam.

"Then I ain't here," Sam said lazily.

Emma put the phone back to her ear. "If you don't identify yourself, I'm afraid

I can't put your call through to Sam," she said icily.

"Ha! Gotcha!" two young, very American voices screamed in Emma's ear.

"This must be Becky and Allie," Emma said dryly.

"We fooled you!" one of the voices said. "Hey, we do English accents really well, huh?"

"Brilliantly," Emma agreed with a smile. Mischievously she pressed the speakerphone button on the telephone so that they could all hear the conversation.

"Jacobs mortuary!" the twins cried together. "You kill 'em, we chill 'em!"

"Hey, guys," Sam replied, her jaw dropping in surprise. "How did you find me here?"

"Are you on a speakerphone?" Allie asked. "You sound funny."

"Yeah," Sam called, sitting up. "Now, how did you monsters track me down?"

"Easy," Becky said.

"We called your parents to wish you happy holidays," Allie reported.

"And they gave us Emma's aunt's number," Becky said.

"So . . . happy holidays!" both girls shouted at once.

Sam grinned, and saw that both Emma and Carrie were smiling, too. She had been through a lot with the twins, but she actually liked them a lot.

"So, merry Christmas," Carrie replied.

"Uh-uh," Becky said.

"We're Jewish," Allie reminded Carrie.

"So, Happy Hanukkah!" Carrie corrected herself a little sheepishly.

"Yo, Sam, what time does the band go onstage?" Becky's voice sounded a little tinny on the speakerphone.

"What?" Sam asked, not comprehending.

"The night after tomorrow," Allie explained. "What time does the band go on?"

"I think eight," Sam replied, trying to recall what Billy had said to them.

"Cool," Becky reported.

"We'll be there," Allie said lightly.

"What?" Sam asked in shock.

"We'll be there," Allie repeated.

"What do you mean, you'll be there?" Sam asked.

"Sam," Becky said, her voice exasperated, "it's only twenty miles away!"

"But—"

"Ha!" Allie cried. "Dad rented a house near Middlebury for the holidays—"

"And we're here," Becky chimed in.

"So we'll see you Wednesday night," Allie concluded.

"You'll get us backstage passes, right?" Becky asked. "The laminated kind?"

It was Carrie who answered first. "You got it," she said.

"Yes!" the twin girls yelled at the same time. "Okay, we'll pick 'em up at the door. Later!"

"So long," Sam said, not knowing quite what else to say.

"Happy Hanukkah, Sam," Becky said, and then she and Allie were gone.

Emma got up and clicked off the telephone.

"Now that was a call I wasn't expecting," she said, plopping down on the floor next to Sam.

"Me neither," Sam replied, putting another log on the fireplace and pushing the burning embers around a bit. "Becky and Allie. I'd almost forgotten about them."

"I doubt it!" Carrie said with a laugh. "Now all we need is for Ian Templeton to call me!"

Ian Templeton was the 13-year-old son of her Sunset Island employer, rock icon Graham Perry Templeton.

The phone rang again.

"No way," Carrie said as Emma got up to answer it. "Can't be Ian . . . can it?"

"Liz Barrington's home, Emma Cresswell speaking," Emma answered again. She listened carefully to the voice on the phone, her eyes widening in surprise.

"Carrie, it's for you," she said.

"Speak of the devil," Sam joked.

"No way," Carrie repeated. "It can't really be Ian!"

Emma handed Carrie the phone without a word, a mischievous smile on her lips.

Carrie sighed and took the phone. It would be just like the twins—who sang in a young teen band Ian had formed on the island—to call Ian to tell him they'd gotten passes to the Flirts' gig.

"I don't believe it!" Carrie exclaimed. She got up and took the phone. "Ian, is that really you?"

Carrie listened for a moment as the person on the other end of the phone spoke to her. A look of surprise crossed her face, followed by a big grin.

"No," Carrie said into the phone, "I am *not* interested in buying aluminum siding! Thank you very much!" She hung up and turned to Emma. "Very funny."

"Gotcha!" Emma said, laughing.

At that moment the front door opened and the guys bustled in, their faces red from the cold.

"Man, it's great out there," Billy said, pulling off his knit cap.

"Hey, Red," Pres called to Sam in a

teasing voice. "Your ready to take a stroll with me?"

"Negative, big guy," Sam said. "It's cold, remember?"

"I'll keep you warm," Pres promised. He walked over to Sam and pulled her up.

"But I'm completely comfortable," Sam whined. "Hey, you hungry? We could pop some popcorn!"

"I've got a better idea," Pres said. Before Sam could ask what the idea was, he had picked her up in his arms.

"Hey, what's the deal?" Sam protested.

"Ever take a Swedish shower?" Pres asked as he carried Sam to the front door.

"Put me down!" Sam yelped. "I'm an indoor kind of babe! Pres! I mean it! Pres!"

The next thing the rest of them heard was Sam screaming as Pres dumped her unceremoniously into the snow.

THREE

"Hey, lovebirds," Sam sang out the next morning when Billy and Carrie entered the kitchen. Everyone else but Erin was already there eating breakfast.

"Mornin'," Billy said with a grin as he and Carrie sidled up to the table. "What's for breakfast?"

"You think there's actually food here for *you?*" Kurt joshed.

Billy and Carrie sat down. "Sure hope so," Billy said. "I'm starving."

"Me too," Carrie chimed in.

Sam groaned. "They sound like they're practically married," she said.

"They practically are," Jake pointed out.

35

Billy and Carrie were the only couple that was sleeping together at the vacation house—they had been in a long-term, committed relationship for two years now.

Otherwise, Sam, Emma, and Erin were sharing one bedroom, Pres and Jake were in another bedroom, and Jay and Kurt had the twin beds upstairs in the small sleeping loft.

And that's about all the room there is, Sam thought. *There's a sofabed, too, but that's it! Good thing the band isn't any bigger.*

Carrie poured herself a cup of coffee from the carafe on the table and surveyed the feast of fresh orange juice, homemade sweet rolls, scrambled eggs, and home-fried potatoes.

"Who made all this?" Carrie asked, helping herself to some juice.

"The chef," Emma said, smiling at Kurt.

"Emma helped," Kurt added.

"Oh, sure," Emma replied with a laugh. "I watched while he made the eggs."

Erin walked into the kitchen and waved lethargically at the group.

"How are you feeling, Erin?" Carrie asked, remembering that Erin's throat had been bothering her.

Erin replied by drawing a finger across her throat and rolling her eyes.

"You can't talk?" Billy asked in alarm.

"Laryngitis," Erin whispered, her voice as small as could be.

"We got us a problem, pardner," Pres drawled. He took a swallow of his orange juice.

Billy reached for a sweet roll, picked it up, and chewed it contemplatively. "No kidding," he said. "Erin, are you totally out of commission?"

Erin nodded sadly.

"Has this happened before?" Billy asked.

Erin nodded.

"How long does it usually last?"

Erin opened her mouth, then apparently thought better of it. She spied a pen and notepad lying on the counter, picked them up, and scrawled a couple of lines. Then she held the pad up.

"A week?" Billy exclaimed.

"Maybe it's only a mild case," Emma said hopefully.

Erin shook her head sadly. "Sorry," she whispered. "It's happened to me before when I get a cold. I wish—"

"Hey, don't strain your voice. It's not your fault," Billy said.

"We can try feeding her vitamin C," Carrie suggested. "I saw some in the medicine cabinet."

Erin shook her head and scribbled another note on the paper.

Won't work, the note read. *I've tried it. Sorry, guys.*

"What are we going to do?" Jay asked, pushing his glasses up his nose.

"Go on without Erin," Pres suggested, "we might could do . . ."

Billy shook his head. "I want three backups," he said emphatically. "Remember, Polimar is coming."

"I'm sure Polimar will understand that—" Emma began.

"Three backups!" Billy repeated firmly.

"Hey, it's not such a biggie, is it?" Sam

asked. "I mean, we already have the deal with Polimar—"

"And so far they've done zero about it," Billy said. "Which is just about as good as having no deal at all."

Carrie gave Billy a sympathetic look. *I know what he's thinking,* she realized. *His older brother, Evan, told Billy that if the Flirts didn't take off soon, Billy was going to have to go back to Seattle to help with his dad's business. He's feeling so pressured. . . .*

"Here's how I see it," Billy said. "Polimar heard us before with three backups, and that's how I want them to hear us again."

"But we don't have three backup singers now," Jake said, running his fingers through his thick, dark hair. Sam could see he felt especially bad for Erin.

I can't believe I once thought that no one could want Erin for a girlfriend because she's overweight, Sam recalled. *Was I wrong. And is Jake awesome-looking!*

"You're serious, man," Pres said to his partner.

"Damn right," Billy growled. "We've got to find another backup singer. Quick."

"Why doesn't Carrie sing?" Emma suggested. "She was great last time." Carrie had briefly sung backup on the Flirts' East Coast tour last summer, when Diana was injured.

"I need a professional voice," Billy said. "A rehearsed, professional voice."

"Well, if not me, who?" Carrie put in. "We have to find someone."

"Anyone but Diana," Sam quipped.

Everyone laughed again.

Everyone but Billy.

"You know, Sam," he said softly, "you might be on to something there."

"You're kidding," Sam said flatly.

"Not necessarily," Billy said slowly.

"No way," Sam said. "She's in, I'm out."

Billy turned to Pres. "She does know all the songs."

"But—" Pres began.

"And the dance combinations," Jay pointed out helpfully. Sam glared at him.

"It's just one night," Billy said. "It's not like she's in the band forever."

40

"You can't be serious," Sam said. "Please, just tell me you're not serious."

"I'm serious," Billy said quietly.

"She'll never do it," Emma said. "Why would she help us?"

"Because she'll be seen by someone from Polimar, that's why," Jay pointed out.

Sam turned to Emma and Carrie. "I can't believe this is happening," she said to her friends. They shrugged helplessly, because they knew the decision was really up to Billy and Pres. Sam buried her head in her hands. "Oh, please, tell me this isn't happening!"

"It would only be one show," Carrie pointed out.

"She's probably off skiing in Switzerland or something," Sam said. "I hope."

Billy shrugged. "Nothing ventured, nothing gained. Who's got her number?"

"Her father's company is De Witt Enterprises in Boston," Emma said.

"You're helping them!" Sam accused Emma as Billy went into the living room to get the phone.

Emma shrugged. "Come on, Sam. I don't like Diana any better than you do, but we have to think about the band."

"And Billy," Carrie added meaningfully.

Sam sighed and shook her head. "She isn't staying here!" she cried. "No matter what!"

Billy came back with the phone. He dialed directory assistance in Massachusetts.

"Boston," he said tersely into the phone. "The number for De Witt Enterprises."

"It could be worse, you know," Carrie said as she got down on her knees and pushed the ball of snow she'd been making another few feet.

"How?" Sam asked. She and Emma were leaning against the big oak tree in the front yard of Emma's Aunt Liz's house.

"Lorell Courtland could be coming, too," Carrie suggested, brushing some excess snow off the huge snowball with a mittened hand.

"How do you know she isn't?" Sam

countered. Lorell was Diana's best friend back on Sunset Island. She was a syrupy-sweet girl from Georgia who was just as hateful to the three of them as Diana was.

"Aren't Diana and her cousin Dee Dee enough?" Carrie asked.

Sam stuck her finger in her mouth and pretended to gag in response.

It was later that afternoon. Erin was resting in bed, Billy and the guys had all gone into town for supplies—and to buy a Christmas tree to put up—and the three friends had decided to take advantage of the relatively warm afternoon by building a snowman in the front yard.

"Maybe Diana's changed," Emma said dubiously.

"Yeah, right," Sam scoffed. "Maybe the Atlantic Ocean is dry."

Billy had been single-minded about finding Diana, and had actually managed to track her down at her father's home in Boston. Then, by a combination of flattery, cajolery, and the promise of a chance to be seen by someone from Polimar Records, he had actually managed to convince Diana to fly in for the gig.

There were only two catches.

First, Diana said that over the holidays she was responsible for her fifteen-year-old cousin, Dee Dee De Witt, so Dee Dee would have to come along, too.

Billy had said okay.

Then, after Billy had made some quick phone calls, they found that every single hotel and motel room within fifty miles was totally booked up. Diana and Dee Dee would have to spend a night with the gang at Aunt Liz's house.

The second catch was that Billy would have to get them back to the airport so they could fly to Hawaii, where their families were spending the rest of the holidays.

Sam had nearly choked when she heard the part about Diana and Dee Dee staying at the cabin.

"Dee Dee," Sam said, picking up some snow and tossing it from hand to hand. "I can't believe it."

"I don't know her that well," Emma

44

said as she leaned over to push her own snowball. "Come help me, okay?"

Sam walked over to where Emma was pushing. "Becky and Allie know her from Club Sunset Island."

"And?" Carrie asked.

"They hate her guts," Sam said. "According to the twins, she's just as bitchy as Diana. She says the meanest things about people, and then tries to pretend she was kidding."

"How awful," Emma sighed.

"Yeah, she's just plain mean. Her and Diana both," Sam agreed. "Maybe it's a genetic thing in the De Witt family. Medical science should study them."

"Let's put this snowman together, you guys," Carrie said, pointing to the three huge snowballs that were lying on the ground.

"Becky and Allie aren't going to be very happy to see Dee Dee at the concert," Emma said, brushing hair out of her eyes with her mittened hand.

"That's the understatement of the year. I hope they and Dee Dee don't kill each other." Sam leaned over to pick up one of the huge snowballs. Then, with a big grunt, she lifted it clear off the ground, placing it very carefully on top of one of the others.

"Muscles," Carrie said admiringly.

"I used to pick up my pet pig," Sam admitted. Carrie and Emma gave her amused looks. "When I was little! And I know what you're thinking. Do *not* rag on my porker."

"I still can't believe you had a pet pig," Emma teased her.

"Pigs happen to be brilliant animals," Sam said with dignity.

The three girls together picked up the last snowball and placed it on top of the other two. Then they quickly and efficiently finished off their creation. Sam had rummaged around in the house's storeroom and had come up with some appropriate summer clothing for the snowman, including a loud Hawaiian shirt and a Red Sox baseball cap. They even laid an empty beer can at his feet.

Sam arranged a broken pair of Ray-

Ban sunglasses on the snowman and stepped back to admire her creation.

"What a babe," she said. "Now he and Diana can get down together."

"Even Diana draws the line somewhere," Carrie said.

"I don't think so," Sam said. "She'll sleep with anyone. So why not a snowman? His heart is as cold as hers!"

"Mistletoe's up!" Kurt called out.

"Okay, big guy," Sam said, poking Pres in the ribs with her toe and reaching down to pull him to his feet, "that's our cue!"

The guys had brought back a fabulous seven-foot-high pine tree, and everyone—Erin included—had spent the afternoon decorating the Christmas tree. In fact, Erin said she was feeling almost back to normal, except for her voice.

Supper—a hearty beef stew, made by Carrie with some help from Emma and Sam—was simmering on the stove, and Kurt had just finished fastening the

47

mistletoe to the ceiling just inside the front door.

Erin scribbled a quick note and thrust it meaningfully at Jake, a sly grin on her face.

"'Just because I can't talk doesn't mean I can't kiss!'" he read aloud, and grinned.

Everyone except for Jay, who was taking a nap, piled into the front hall.

"Who's first?" Kurt asked.

No one volunteered. And then Erin held up her scribbled sign.

Me, it read.

She took Jake by the hand, and the two of them walked directly under the mistletoe. She opened her arms. Jake moved close to her and kissed her passionately.

"Wow!" Sam exclaimed. Everyone laughed and then applauded good-naturedly.

After Erin and Jake came up for air, first Billy and Carrie, and then Kurt and Emma, took their turn under the mistletoe. Each couple got the same "wow" from Sam and applause from the others.

"You ready, big guy?" Sam asked when it was her and Pres's turn.

"You betcha," Pres drawled. He drew Sam toward him. As she moved into his embrace Sam sighed at the feel of his arms around her. She closed her eyes. And then she felt a quick peck on the lips.

She opened her eyes. "That was it?"

Pres nodded.

"All of it?" Sam asked.

Pres nodded again.

"Well, then, all I have to say is, you're slipping," Sam remarked, folding her arms.

"And all I have to say is, I like to do my kissing in private," Pres explained, drawing her to one side, a little away from the others.

"But everyone else just put on this big public display of affection!" Sam protested. "They're gonna think you don't love me!"

Pres took Sam by the hand and led her into the living room. "Now," he said.

"Now?" she whispered. "But we're all alone!"

"That's the idea," Pres said.

"And there's no mistletoe," Sam added.

But Pres just pressed his lips to hers, and soon Sam forgot all about everything except for that perfect kiss.

FOUR

"Sam?" Carrie said when she saw her friend sitting alone in the living room, staring at the Christmas tree. "Are you okay?"

"I'm fine," Sam said, the tone of her voice flat. "Just fine."

Carrie walked in and sat beside her friend on the couch. "You don't sound fine, Sam," she said. "Not at all."

It was the next afternoon, the day before the big Flirts show. Everyone else had gone to the mall in Burlington to do some last-minute holiday shopping, but Carrie had already finished her shopping before the trip, and Sam had said she didn't feel like going. No amount of cajoling from her friends could convince her, so they had left without her.

"So, what's up?" Carrie asked.

"Nothing."

"Sam, you can't fool me."

"Sure I can," Sam said, trying to make a joke. "I'm great at fooling you."

Carrie just stared at her with concern. *I can't imagine what's wrong. She seemed to be having such a great time here with everybody. I can't believe that Diana's coming here would upset her as much as this.*

Sam sighed, and Carrie grew more concerned. "Is it Diana?" Carrie ventured.

Sam's smile was faint. "Nope," she replied. "You think I'd be bummed out over De Bitch?"

"You're sure it's not Diana?"

"Why should I worry about Diana?" Sam asked, pointing out the living room window at the snowman they'd built the day before. "She has our snowman friend."

Carrie smiled. "Well," she said, "whatever it is, you know I'm here to listen."

Sam sighed again, and then reached forward to pick up a handful of Doritos from a bowl that was on the coffee table in front of her.

That's a good sign, Carrie thought. *If she's eating Doritos by the handful, that's still the Sam I know and love!*

"I see you haven't lost your taste for Doritos," Carrie said. "Life can't be that bad."

"Oh, I'd eat if I was dying," Sam said between chews. She reached for her glass of Coke and took a long gulp, then set it back on the coffee table. "I'll tell you what's the matter."

"Yes?" Carrie prompted her.

"It's Christmas."

"Christmas?" Carrie repeated. "You're upset that it's Christmas?"

"I've been thinking about Christmas," Sam continued, taking another Dorito and chewing it thoughtfully.

"What about it?" Carrie said.

"I'm not sure I can explain it," Sam said, her forehead wrinkled in thought.

"It's just that I've got the weirdest feeling this year."

I really am not at all sure what she's talking about, Carrie thought. *What's especially weird about Christmas this year? I love Christmas! It's such a great family—*

And then it came to her.

"You're thinking about your family," Carrie suggested gently.

Sam nodded.

"You're sad that you're not spending Christmas with your family in Kansas?" Carrie asked.

"Sort of, kind of," Sam said. "But it's more than that."

"How so?"

"I don't even know who my family is anymore," Sam said a little wistfully.

"What do you mean?" Carrie asked. She unconsciously picked up a Dorito, too.

"Well, my mom and dad and sister in Kansas are all celebrating Christmas together," Sam began.

"And you feel bad because you're not there," Carrie ventured.

"A little," Sam said, getting up to put another log on the fire.

"I don't understand," Carrie said, puzzled.

"Look," Sam said, giving the fire a poke and sitting back down next to her friend. "What would you do if you knew that you were adopted by a couple that celebrates Christmas, and you always celebrated Christmas with them, and then you found out later that your birth mother and your birth father are Jewish and don't celebrate Christmas at all?"

Carrie was silent. "I see what you mean," she finally said.

"I don't know the right thing to do," Sam confessed.

"A lot of my Jewish friends at Yale celebrate Hanukkah," Carrie ventured. "You could, too."

Sam shrugged. "I know about Hanukkah," she said. "I'm just confused, that's all. I mean, can you be Jewish and celebrate Christmas?"

"I don't know," Carrie said honestly. "I guess you could ask your birth mother. You like Susan. You could talk to her about what you're feeling."

"Yeah, I could," Sam said with a sigh. "I tell you, though, it's a weird feeling."

"It's not easy," Carrie sympathized. She was silent for a moment. "You don't have to choose, you know," she went on. "I mean, you can love your parents *and* your birth parents without betraying anybody."

"You think?" Sam asked.

"Sure. I really don't think Susan would be insulted that you celebrate Christmas," Carrie said. "Neither would your birth father. I mean, Michael knows that's how you were raised."

"Yeah, I guess," Sam agreed.

"On the other hand, if you wanted to learn more about Hanukkah and celebrate both, I think that would kind of integrate both parts of you, you know?" Carrie suggested.

Sam grinned. "You are amazing, Car. I feel better already, just talking about it with you. You should be a shrink."

"No thanks," Carrie said, looking out the window at the fading light of the afternoon. "I'll stick to taking pictures."

"One thing," Sam said.

"What's that?"

"Taking pictures is cool," Sam told her. "So long as it's always *my* picture you're taking!"

"What's that noise?" Kurt asked.

"What noise?" Emma replied.

"I don't hear anything," Jay said.

"Shh!" Kurt shushed everyone.

It was around eight o'clock that night— an absolutely magnificent winter night, with a perfectly clear sky, a completely full moon, and temperatures in the mid-twenties. Erin and Jake had prepared homemade pizza for everyone, and now, as had become the routine at the house, everyone was gathered in the living room around the fireplace, just talking.

"Now do you hear it, Emma?" Kurt asked.

"I still don't hear a thing," she told him.

"Quiet!" Kurt insisted. "There it is!"

Everyone quieted quickly. And this time they all *could* hear it: the sound of bells ringing, ever so softly, coming from outside.

Kurt rushed to the living room window and peered off into the distance.

"Hey!" he shouted. "There's a big sleigh coming this way!"

Everyone except for Emma jumped up and rushed over to the window to see. Carrie turned and looked at Emma, who gave her a sly wink.

The horse-drawn sleigh approached them, its sleigh bells getting louder and louder, until it came to a stop right outside the house.

"Who's interested in a sleigh ride?" Emma asked innocently.

"A sleigh ride?" Sam cried. "Now, that's romance!" She poked Pres gently in the ribs. "You're a pretty romantic kind of guy, even if you hate to kiss in public!"

The man sitting on the sleigh gave a few quick tugs on the bells again.

"Sleigh's **leaving in ten minutes,**"

Emma announced. "I suggest everyone get dressed!"

Ten minutes later, everyone had hastily pulled on all the warm gear they could find and hopped into the sleigh. They covered themselves with the warm woolen blankets they found there as the horse-drawn sleigh pulled them through the snow.

"I've got to hand it to you, Emma," Kurt said, drawing Emma closer to him underneath the blanket they'd draped over their laps. "You had me fooled. How did you pull this off?"

Emma smiled happily. "Actually, it's a gift to all of us from Aunt Liz," she said. "She called me just before she left and told me she'd arranged it all!"

"It's a fantastic idea!" Carrie exclaimed.

Emma was delighted her friends were having such a good time. *Aunt Liz has to be the greatest aunt anyone could have,* she thought.

"Jingle bells, jingle bells," Pres started to sing, and then, one by one, all of them except Erin joined in on the famous song about a sleigh ride. Emma and Sam sang harmony. Their voices got louder and louder, and Emma could actually see some lights get flicked on in rooms of homes around the lake, as people went to their windows to see who was singing.

"This is the best Christmas ever," Kurt fervently whispered to Emma when the last song was over.

"I agree," Emma said, taking Kurt's hand in her own and squeezing it warmly.

"We'll need to do this more often," Kurt wrapped his arm more tightly around Emma.

"It's perfect," she agreed. "The night, the snow, the moon . . ."

"And you." Kurt kissed Emma gently on the cheek.

"Your dad isn't upset with you because you're spending Christmas here?" Emma asked.

Kurt sighed. "Every since my mom died . . . well, Christmas has never been the same for him."

"That's so sad," Emma whispered. "Next

Christmas, let's both spend it with him, okay?"

"I love you, Emma," he whispered back, and kissed her again. "How about your mom? Is she mad?"

"I think Kat wishes I were home," Emma admitted, her voice a little sad. "But I think it's important that you and I be together now."

Kurt nodded.

If only she would just see, Emma thought as images of the terrible fight she'd had last summer with her mother over Kurt came flooding back to her. *If only she'd just see what a great guy Kurt is, and not just that he comes from a poor family! She forced me to choose between the family millions and Kurt. I bet she never thought I'd actually choose Kurt. . . . Maybe someday Dad will convince her that I shouldn't be cut off financially until I turn 21. But if I had to do it all over again, I'd still choose Kurt.*

"Did I thank you recently?" Kurt asked.

"For what?" Emma answered.

"For standing by me last summer,"

Kurt murmured quietly, so no one else on the sleigh would hear. He didn't have to worry—everyone else was busy talking, or just lying back under their warm blankets, admiring the stars.

Emma blushed, hoping that in the dark Kurt wouldn't notice. "You don't have to thank me," she whispered. "Kurt, I—"

"Shush," Kurt quieted her. "Don't say anything else." He leaned over and kissed Emma again, and the kiss was so sweet and deep that it took Emma's breath away.

"There," Kurt continued when the kiss was over. "I think that says it better than anything."

"I agree." Emma smiled and snuggled against Kurt's shoulder.

"Look!" Pres called out softly. "Look over there!"

Emma and Kurt sat up to see what Pres was pointing to. Over to the right of the sleigh, about two hundred yards away, stood deer, perfectly illuminated by the moonlight that reflected off the white **snow. The deer were nibbling the bark off** the lower branches of a small tree at the edge of the lake, seemingly without a care in the world.

"They're so beautiful," Emma said softly.

"Not as beautiful as you," Kurt commented.

"You're a little biased," Emma said, and kissed his cheek.

If we hadn't endured the difficult times we've had, she wondered, *would we still feel so strongly about each other as we do now?*

She never got a chance to answer that question, though, because Kurt leaned over and kissed her one more time.

The driver of the sleigh finally pulled to a stop. The night was clear and beautiful. Their breath made puffs of steamy air come out of their mouths.

"I'm amazed we haven't startled them away," Carrie said to Emma in a low voice.

"They're hungry," Emma said.

"That's right," Billy added. "They have to take the risk."

Carrie looked at Billy. "Kind of like you with Polimar, huh?"

"What do you mean?" Billy asked. Emma looked on curiously.

"Inviting Diana for tomorrow night," Carrie explained. "You're hungry enough to take the risk."

"She'll be okay," Billy said.

"I hope so," Carrie said, still watching the deer. *I really hope so,* she added in her mind. *Because for us to trust Diana is like that deer trusting a human.*

Who might have a loaded gun.

FIVE

"I'm not nervous," Sam said as she stared into a small mirror. "I'm getting a zit on my chin, but I'm not nervous."

Sam, Emma, and Carrie were all relaxing before the Flirts' big show in the small dressing room backstage at the concert hall. The furniture in the room consisted of two old couches, a couple of battered tables, and some chairs with the stuffing falling out of them. There was a sad-looking plant drooping in the corner, and someone had written "Water me" on the wall above it.

"You never get pimples," Emma said as she checked to make sure she wasn't getting a run in the left leg of her panty-hose.

"Better make that 'hardly ever,'" Sam said, peering at her face. "Now I'll probably get my period, too, just to make my life complete."

The Flirts' big show was to begin in about an hour and a half. The band had been told to expect a good-sized crowd; though some clouds had been building throughout the day, no snow had fallen to prevent people from coming to the show.

As planned, they had all driven to the Burlington concert hall in caravan for a short rehearsal and sound check. Diana DeWitt, along with her fifteen-year-old cousin Dee Dee, had arrived that afternoon and met them at the club.

For once, Diana hadn't immediately started in with her little digs and nasty comments. Mostly she just gave the other girls totally supercilious looks as Billy had the band run through the songs they would play that evening.

Diana actually remembered the dance

combinations, Sam thought. *I've got to hand it to her. She's not without talent. Even if she is a total bitch.*

"If it's Dee Dee at the door you have my permission to shoot her," Carrie called.

"I'll be a character witness for your defense," Emma added. "No jury would dare convict you."

If Diana had been silent and snobby since she'd arrived, her cousin Dee Dee had completely redefined the word *obnoxious.*

She'd criticized everything, from the Flirts' lyrics to the girls' stage outfits, punctuating every nasty, critical remark with an offhand "I was only kidding. Can't you guys take a joke?"

As Sam was reflecting, there came a timid knock on the door.

"I'll get it," Sam offered, getting up off the couch and walking across the room toward the door.

"If it's Cody Leete," Carrie reminded her, "Billy said to tell him that he'll meet **him in the sound booth.**"

"Yeah, I remember," Sam said. "But I bet you the guy'll be late."

"It's his record company," Carrie reminded her. "Be nice."

"*Moi?*" Sam asked as she pulled open the door. "I'm always nice."

A girl Sam didn't recognize was standing there alone, a forlorn expression on her face. She looked about fourteen.

"Hi," the girl said in a thin voice.

"Hi," Sam replied, looking at the slight, short girl quizzically. Her pretty face was pale and delicate. She had very short hair that was dyed an array of colors—brown, blond, and purple. Her large brown eyes gazed at Sam. She was dressed in typical grunge style—combat boots, battered jeans, a T-shirt with a photo of Kurt Cobain on it, and a brown and white long-sleeved flannel shirt.

"Can I help you?" Sam queried.

"Is this the Flirts' dressing room?" the girl asked, her eyes growing even larger. "The guard said it was."

"Yeah," Sam replied, not knowing what

to make of the teen. "How'd you get back here? You have a pass?"

The girl just stood there, not saying anything, shrugging slightly.

"So what's the deal?" Sam said. "What do you want?"

"I'm Tina," the girl said. "I totally love the Flirts."

"Uh-huh," Sam said, leaning against the door frame. *As if that explains everything,* she thought wryly.

The girl peered around Sam. "Are they in there?"

"I'm part of the Flirts," Sam explained.

"No way," the girl insisted.

"I am," Sam said. "I sing backup."

"I'm talking about the *real* Flirts," the girl said earnestly. "Billy. Pres. Jay. Sly."

Sam turned to Emma and Carrie. They shared a measured look. Evidently this girl didn't know that Sly was dead.

Sam turned back to the young girl. "They're not here right now—"

"I drove up here from New Hampshire," Tina interrupted. "To see the show."

"Alone?" Sam asked her. The girl was

obviously too young to have a driver's license. *I bet she hitched*, Sam thought.

"No," Tina answered. "With friends."

"Where are they?"

Tina waved her hand behind her. "Somewhere back there," she said non-committally. "Look, are the guys in the band going to be back soon?"

"You know, they're really busy right now," Sam began.

"I'm not a groupie or anything, if that's what you're thinking," Tina said. "I mean, I didn't come here to, like, have sex with them or something."

"Gee, that's a relief," Sam said sarcastically. "Look, I'm glad you're a fan, and I hope you enjoy the show. But we've got to get ready now." She started to close the door.

"Hey!" Tina called. "Wait a sec!"

Sam opened the door again. Tina pulled a tiny instant camera out of her pocket.

"Can I, like, take your picture?" she asked. "I mean, for my scrapbook. You really do sing with the band, right? You're not just someone's girlfriend or some-thing?"

"I'm with the band," Sam said huffily.

"Yeah, I kind of remember you, I think," Tina said eagerly. "Wow, that must be so rad."

"Yeah," Sam agreed. "It is." She opened the door a little wider. "My friend Emma over there sings backup, too. And that's Carrie Alden. She's the band's photographer."

"Can I take pictures of all of you?" Tina asked eagerly. "It'd mean so much to me. I love the Flirts."

Sam glanced at Emma and Carrie, who nodded approval.

"Okay," Sam said.

Sam invited Tina into the dressing room, where the teen snapped a couple of photos of the three friends sitting together on the couch.

When she was done, she stood there expectantly.

"You're going to have to leave now," Carrie said, her voice kind. "The guys will be coming back soon to get ready."

71

"Cool," Tina commented. She didn't move.

"She means it," Sam said. "You gotta boogie."

"Sure, no prob," Tina agreed. "Hey, can I take a picture of your van?"

"Excuse me?" Emma asked.

"The band's van," Tina said. "Outside. It's the blue one, right?"

"No, it's the green one with the Maine plates," Sam corrected her.

"Thanks!" Tina said. "I'll see you guys later." At the door she turned back to look at them. "Hey, say hi to the guys from me, okay? Tina from Brenford, New Hampshire? You'll tell them?"

"Sure," Sam agreed, and she closed the door behind the girl.

"She can't be more than fourteen years old," Emma said.

"If that," Carrie added.

"Jeez," Sam said, plopping down on the couch. "You think she hitched here alone?"

Carrie shrugged. "Probably. I'll bet that line about driving up with some friends was a big lie."

"I feel sorry for her," Emma said softly. "Do you think she's okay?"

"I wonder where her parents are," Carrie mused.

"Where most parents are whose kids take off," Sam said with a shrug. "Not paying attention."

"You never did it?" Carrie asked Sam.

"In Junction, Kansas?" Sam asked. "Please! Everyone knew me! They'd just pick me up and take me back home. There was no easy escape!"

"It's a shame," Carrie said thoughtfully. "The kid needs help."

"Carrie," Sam chided, "you can't mother the entire world."

"But she's just a baby!" Carrie exclaimed.

"Yeah, right," Sam said. "She's probably done more and seen more than you have, girlfriend."

"Well, if that's true, don't you think it's sad?" Emma asked, reaching into her bag for some breath mints.

"You guys are jumping to all sorts of conclusions," Sam said. "She didn't seem

73

strung out on drugs, she wasn't drunk—maybe she's just fine!"

"I don't think so," Emma said quietly, popping a mint into her mouth.

"I'll tell you what would make her want to go home right away," Sam remarked.

"What's that?" Emma asked.

"Set her up to watch the show with Dee Dee De Witt!" Sam cracked.

Neither Carrie nor Emma laughed. Their minds were still on Tina.

No, I bet her parents don't know where she is, Sam thought. *She probably just sneaked away. Or lied and said she was at a friend's house. That's what I would have done. I just hope Tina isn't as dumb as I was at fourteen!*

"Sam!" Allie Jacobs yelled at the top of her lungs.

"Yo, Sam!" her sister, Becky, screamed.

Sam turned around. She'd gone down the hall to find the bathroom. As predicted, she had gotten her period.

"Becky! Allie!" she cried.

I can't believe it, Sam thought as the two girls, all-access backstage passes hanging around their necks, ran over to her, jumped up, and hugged her. *I am actually glad to see them! See what a few hours with Dee Dee will do to a person?* she thought wryly.

"We're so pumped!" Allie called.

"We couldn't believe it when we read about it in the paper, " Becky chimed in.

"We made Dad bring us," Allie said.

"He didn't want to, but we convinced him," Becky said proudly.

"You guys look great," Sam said, surveying their outfits.

"Thanks," Becky said. "We put the unis together just for you."

Becky was wearing a short black dress with a flannel shirt knotted at the waist over it. On her feet were combat boots, and a chain of plastic daisies was wrapped around her right ankle. Allie was wearing shocking-pink oversized jean overalls over a long-sleeved pale pink T-shirt. On her feet were high-top sneakers covered with Minnie Mouses.

"Hey, those are my sneakers!" Sam told her.

"You left 'em at the house on the island," Allie said with a shrug. "All you ever wear are your red cowboy boots, anyway."

"Well, I want 'em back soon, anyway," Sam warned. "Is your dad here?"

"He and Kiki dropped us off," Allie said.

"Thank God," Becky added fervently. "They went to the movies. They'll be back later."

"Dan's still with Kiki?" Sam asked.

Allie stuck out her tongue, while Becky reached for her throat and pretended to gag. Sam laughed at their reaction.

"If it were you, you wouldn't be laughing," Becky pointed out.

"You've got a point there," Sam said, admiring Becky's logic.

Kiki Coors was a young actress whom Dan had met the summer before on Sunset Island. Actually, Becky and Allie were responsible for the meeting, because they'd hired Kiki to play the role of their mother for Parents' Day at Club Sunset Island. Since their mother had split a long time before and their father was going out of town, they'd thought Kiki could pretend to be their mom.

They'd been too successful. Not only had Kiki played their mom on Parents' Day, but she and Dan Jacobs had met and started dating. Kiki had practically become a member of the family, bossing Becky and Allie around as though they were her kids.

"How is she?" Sam asked.

"Worse," Becky answered.

"Double worse," Allie chimed in. "Just today she—"

"Well, well, well," came a voice from out of the shadows. "Lookie who's here."

Dee Dee De Witt, also sporting a backstage pass, stood in the doorway. Her dress was so short it made Becky's dress look modest. It was made of stretch white lace and you could see her bikini underwear right through the dress.

"*You're* here?" Becky gasped.

"I can't believe it," Allie said, shaking

her head in disgust. "When did you get here?"

"When did *you* get here?" Dee Dee commented, approaching the twins and looking them up and down. "I see you didn't have time to dress."

"What's wrong with our outfits?" Allie asked defensively.

"They're so juvenile," Dee Dee said. "You look like you're about ten years old."

"Do not," Becky said.

"Oh, get over it," Dee Dee snapped. "I was only joking!"

"I'd almost forgotten how awful you are," Becky said, a cold edge to her voice.

"How's your friend? You know, the fat one? The one who looks like a guy?" Dee Dee asked. "What's her name? Boring Lakeland?"

"Tori," Allie said sharply. "And she's not fat."

"I was only kidding," Dee Dee said. "Can't you take a joke?"

"Dee Dee," Sam began, "maybe you should leave now."

"Are you kidding?" Dee Dee said. "I'm

older than you, and I was here first." She planted both feet firmly on the ground.

"Maybe *we* should leave," Sam suggested instead, touching the twins lightly on their arms and starting to steer them away.

The twins took the hint, and they left without saying good-bye to Dee Dee.

"What a witch!" Allie cried when they were out of earshot.

"I hated her last summer," Becky recalled.

"I hate her more now," Allie said.

"What's she doing here?" Becky demanded.

Sam quickly explained about Erin's laryngitis, and how Diana was in the show.

"No!" Allie cried. "You actually invited Diana? She's out to get all of you!"

"Look, it wasn't up to me," Sam said. "Anyway, so far Diana has been almost decent. Dee Dee's been much nastier than Diana."

"She has to be plotting something, then," Becky said darkly.

"Look, let's just chill out about them, okay?" Sam suggested. "You two go out there and enjoy the show."

Allie gave her an arch look. "With Dee Dee and Diana in the same state? Are you kidding?"

"Why, Sam, I can't believe a girl as flat-chested as you ever got a guy like Pres!" Allie crooned in an imitation of Dee Dee. "Jeez, I'm only kidding. Can't you take a joke?"

"Yeah," Becky echoed, picking up on Allie's imitation. "It's too bad you're not as perfect as I am! Perfectly bitchy, that is!"

Both girls cracked up, and finally Sam could resist no longer. All three of them stood, laughing together as if it was still summer and they were back in that magical place called Sunset Island, Maine.

SIX

"Ladies and gentlemen," boomed the loudspeaker, "the Rock Spot is proud to present Polimar recording artists Flirting With Danger!"

A huge roar went up from the capacity crowd in the concert hall.

And no wonder. They'd been kept waiting for an hour with only prerecorded rock and roll to amuse them. The warm-up band that was scheduled to play had turned out to be a no-show, and then there were various problems with the sound system.

From time to time the crowd had tried to get the show going with spontaneous, rhythmic clapping. Now, finally, the Flirts were taking the stage, and the crowd vented its pent-up emotion.

Emma and Sam, holding hands, ran out to their places, with Diana following. The guys sprinted out right behind them.

I love this, Emma thought as she took her position between Diana and Sam in front of the roaring crowd. *I may not be a rock-and-roll singer forever, but it sure is great to be able to do this for at least a little while!*

The noise from the crowd got even louder, and the rhythmic clapping started again, slowly at first, then quicker and quicker. Jake played an improvised fast riff on his drums in counterpoint.

"Hey, Vermont, wazzup?" Billy growled into the mike. "Are you ready to rock and roll? Let's hit it!"

Billy swung his arm into the air, and at just the right moment on its downward arc, Jake hit four hard beats on his drums. Then Billy joined in, ripping off four measures of moaning guitar, and the band plunged into their signature song, "Love Junkie."

You want too much
And you want too fast
You don't know nothin'
About making love last.
You're a love tornado
That's how you get your kicks
You use me up
And move on to your next fix. . . .

You're a Love Junkie
A Love Junkie, baby
A Love Junkie
You're drivin' me crazy. . . .

At the end of the first verse, Emma,
Sam, and Diana did their patented spin
move and sang, "Love, love junkie, baby!"
into their mikes. The crowd went nuts,
screaming the chorus out as one. When
the chorus was over, Emma sneaked a
quick glance at Sam, who nodded.

Then Emma looked at Diana, on her
other side. *I've got to hand it to Diana,*
she thought. *She's performing as though
she never missed a rehearsal.*

When the song snapped to an end, the

crowd cheered, clapped, and shouted. Diana turned and saw Emma looking at her. She gave Emma an egotistic smirk.

Diana waved to the crowd. "I forgot how much fun this is," she said.

"You were really good," Emma said honestly.

"Of course," Diana said smoothly, adjusting the narrow strap of her white fringed dress. "I always was. Maybe you just forgot."

The three girls were wearing their original Flirts costumes—white fringed numbers from the sixties they had found in a thrift shop. Erin's stage outfits would have been way too big for size-four Diana.

"Cody Leete, are you listening?" Sam called out—fortunately not into her mike.

"Sam!" Emma said quickly. "Look!" She pointed out into the crowd.

"Whoa, baby! Coolness!" Sam responded, pointing also. "Check it out!"

"All right!" Billy yelled into his mike when he saw what Sam and Emma were pointing at. Out in the audience, floating slowly toward the ceiling, hoisted by four or five helium balloons on a string, was an eight-foot by three-foot banner that read, Sunset Island and Flirts Rule!

"Becky and Allie," Sam called to Emma. "It has to be them!"

"Well it sure isn't Dee Dee," Diana said, overhearing Sam's comment. "She wouldn't do something so . . . so tacky!"

"I think it's darling," Emma said loyally.

"You would," Diana put in, hissing the words between her teeth as she smiled for the crowd.

"All right!" Billy yelled again, catching another glimpse of the floating sign as the lighting operator shone a spotlight directly on it. "Sunset Island rules, but Vermont's right up there, too!" The crowd yelled back its approval.

"Vermont, you take my breath away!" Billy shouted in response, and the band raced into its next song.

> Each and every day
> You take my breath away.

What more can I say,
You take my breath away.

I try to find a way,
There's no game I won't play
But what more can I say,
You take my breath away.

At the instrumental break, Emma, Sam, and Diana sang the words "Take my breath, take my breath" two times, and then all three girls, by prearrangement, engaged in a little bit of theater.

Emma ran up to Billy, Sam went over to Pres, and Diana stepped to Jay's side. The three of them kissed their guys on the cheek at the same time, and each guy faked a fainting spell.

The crowd loved it.

For the rest of the night, the crowd was firmly in the Flirts' musical hands.

"Whoa, that was something else, huh?" Sam said happily as she gathered up her stuff from the dressing room. "Let's see, what did I leave behind?"

"Talent?" Diana suggested sweetly as she dropped her cosmetics into her bag.

"Gee, life was just so boring without you around," Sam said sarcastically.

"You have to admit, I was really good tonight," Diana said.

"Okay," Sam said grudgingly.

"You're very talented," Emma agreed. "Which has nothing at all to do with what kind of human being you are."

"Gee, I'm really cut by that," Diana said with a laugh. "I'll be staying up nights worrying." She picked up a tube of lipstick and applied some, then dropped it into her bag. "Who's better, me or the cow?"

"Her name is Erin," Sam said through clenched teeth.

"Yeah, like you don't secretly think of her as the cow, too," Diana said.

"Why do you enjoy being so nasty?" Emma asked. "I really don't understand it."

"Look, the way I see it is this," Diana said. "Some people are just more fake than other people. They pretend to be all

87

sweetness and light, but they'll stab you in the back the moment you turn around. I don't believe in being a hypocrite, that's all. So, who's better, me or—"

"Her name is Erin," Emma reminded Diana.

"Whatever," Diana said. "Who's better?"

"You're both really good," Emma said. "I'd say her singing is a little stronger, and your dancing might be a little stronger."

"And I look a hell of a lot better," Diana pointed out.

"That is a matter of opinion," Sam said, zipping up her own bag. "I don't see Jake going out with you."

"It must be some kind of mercy thing," Diana mused. "Or maybe he's one of those chubby chasers—you know, sickos who go after fat chicks."

"You're the sicko," Sam said, making a face.

"Look, my point is this," Diana said briskly. "The band is better with me in it.

It looks better, it *is* better. I should be back in the band."

Emma and Sam looked at Diana in shock.

"You want to be back in the Flirts?" Emma finally asked.

Diana shrugged. "I'm just saying that you'd have a much better shot with me, okay?"

"Erin is in the band now, not you," Sam said. "Case closed."

"Hey, Sam, guess what?" Diana said. "It's not your decision."

"Right," Sam agreed. "It's Billy and Pres's decision. Which I'm sure is exactly the same as my decision."

"We'll see about that," Diana said, a knowing look on her face.

Once the girls had finished changing and had checked the dressing room one last time, they met up with the others in the hallway and headed toward the stage door.

"Oh, hi, Erin," Diana said nastily. Erin had come to the show; she'd hung out with Carrie as she took photos.

Erin waved, since she still couldn't talk easily.

"Listen, a girl with your figure problems shouldn't be wearing tight jeans," Diana said. "I hope you don't mind my little fashion tip."

"I think she looks great," Jake said, putting his arm around Erin.

"Better get your eyes checked, then," Diana said, shaking her chestnut curls off her face.

"Diana, shut up," Sam said. She and the others were heading for the stage door. Sam opened it and stepped outside. "Wow!"

The entire world was white.

"Dang," Pres marveled. "We don't get weather like this in Tennessee."

"Now I know why Dad hasn't come to pick us up," Allie Jacobs remarked.

The rest of the band pushed out the door, and they all stood there staring.

Despite the weather forecasters' prediction that the snowfall, if any, would be extremely light, a sudden snowstorm had arisen, and it was now snowing harder than any of them had ever seen it snow in their lives. Even Kurt, who'd grown up in Maine and had seen a lot of heavy snow, was stunned.

There were eight inches already on the ground, and the night sky was a sheet of white. Visibility was down to almost zero. It was almost like standing inside a Ping-Pong ball.

It was now a couple of hours after the show had ended, and the parking lot was practically empty. The band had hung out in the dressing room after the show, eating sandwiches Kurt had picked up earlier and talking with Cody Leete (who had finally shown up), the Jacobs twins, and various other hangers-on.

Cody Leete actually said he thought we were good tonight, Sam remembered. *He told Billy that he thought we'd be recording in a month or two. And then he left. Too bad he didn't come back to tell us that we ought to think about leaving, too.*

Nobody had been outside, and nobody had thought to tell the band that the weather had changed in a big way.

"What are we gonna do?" Becky asked plaintively, shielding her face with her hand from the blowing snow.

"Yeah, Sam," Allie added. "What's the deal?"

Why are they asking me? Sam thought. *I'm not their au pair now. Their dad isn't paying me to take care of them!* "I don't know," she said, looking at Emma as if she'd have the answer. Emma just shrugged helplessly.

"Aunt Liz's place isn't that far," she said. "But . . ."

Her voice trailed off. The snow was really coming down. Emma couldn't tell the difference between the roadways and the side of the road.

"What are we gonna do?" Allie asked, and Emma could detect a note of real panic in her voice.

She made a quick decision. "You're going to come with us," she said.

"And go where?" Becky asked.

"Back to my aunt's house," Emma told her, "and we'll just call your dad from there, okay?"

Becky and Allie looked at each other, unsure. Then Becky spoke up.

"Sure," she agreed hesitantly. "I guess there's no way our dad could get through to us here."

"That's assumin' we ever get out of here," Pres said contemplatively. He drew the scarf he was wearing more tightly around the collar of his leather jacket and stared out into the whiteness. "I've never seen anything like this!"

"Hold on, hold on, hold on," Dee Dee said, putting her hands on her hips. "Are you telling me I'm going to have to spend a night with Becky and Allie Jacobs? What if I catch whatever it is that makes them so incredibly lame?"

"Dee Dee, why don't you go for a walk in the snow and forget to come back?" Allie suggested acidly.

"Oh, chill," Dee Dee responded. "Can't you take a joke?"

"Look, the twins are only going to be there until their dad comes—"

"Which better be soon," Becky put in, "or else I'm going to kill Dee Dee—"

"Cut it out!" Billy commanded the younger kids, and they immediately fell silent. "I don't want to hear this crap now!" Billy had a worried look on his face. Clearly he didn't see an easy way out of their predicament with the weather.

Just then a Burlington municipal truck, its snowplow blade lowered, pulled around the side of the building and up toward the stage door. Two guys were sitting in the front seat, orange hunting caps perched on their heads.

"You the band that played tonight?" the driver called to Sam and her friends.

"You got it," Billy yelled back. "And we're gonna be here tomorrow night, too, if we don't get out of here."

"Can y'all help us out?" Pres drawled. "I'm not used to all this snow, and I sure would like to get out of here."

The driver gave them a thoughtful nod. "How many vehicles in your group?" he queried.

Emma did a quick calculation. There was the band's van and a couple of other cars. *Six or seven of us can fit in the van,* she thought. *The rest of us can go in the other two cars. I know we've all got front-wheel drive.*

"Three," she said.

The two guys in the snowplow truck conferred with each other for a couple of moments as Emma and her friends looked on.

"We're going to do you a favor," the driver said. "How far away are you stay-ing?"

"On Long Lake," Emma explained. "About ten miles down Route 7."

The men in the truck conferred some more. Finally they turned back to Emma and her friends.

"Don't you dare tell anyone we're doing this," one said to Emma. "We're supposed to be plowing our assigned streets now. But our boys were at your band's show tonight."

"They loved it," the other man said.

"So we're going to give you an escort home," the driver explained. "We'll just put the plow down."

An impromptu cheer went up from the group—even Dee Dee shouted for joy.

"I don't know how to thank you," Emma said.

"I do," the driver said with a grin. "How about a signed photo of the band?" he asked, addressing his question to Billy. "Sign it, 'To Tom, Mike, and their dad, who saved our butts'!"

Billy grinned. "You got it," he said. "You want it now or later?"

"Do it later," the driver advised. "Let me actually save your butts first!"

SEVEN

Allie and Becky Jacobs were the last two people out of the van.

Or so Emma thought. Because after the twins had climbed out and had begun stretching their stiff legs, *another* teenage girl, this one wrapped in a blanket, also stepped down out of the vehicle, her feet sinking into the deep snow.

"Who on earth are you?" Billy asked the girl. He sounded extremely surprised.

"I'm—"

"Wait," Emma said, still a little bewildered by this peculiar turn of events. "I know her!"

Emma and her friends had just finished the treacherous drive from the concert hall back to Aunt Liz's house. And if it hadn't been for the municipal truck driving in front of them, they might never have made it. All along the highway, there were cars that had skidded off the road, or had just been abandoned. The highway conditions were, to say the least, awful.

Pres, Billy, Erin, Jake, and the twins now gathered around. They were all staring at the young girl, who evidently had been completely hidden in the back of the van as they had carefully made their way along Route 7 toward Aunt Liz's vacation home.

The knot of people was eerily lit by the headlights of the other two cars in their group, which were slowly coming down the snow-covered dirt road toward them.

God, after that ride, now this? Emma thought frantically. *That was one of the scariest car rides in my life. If it weren't for the truck, we'd still be at the club. But where am I going to put all these people? A few hours ago there were four girls and five guys. Now there are five girls, five guys, and four kids.*

What are we going to eat? Where are they all going to sleep? Do I have enough toilet paper?

"Her name is Tina," Emma said. She gestured to the girl, who stood in the snow, her arms folded in front of her, shivering slightly in her thin coat. "Tina, this is—"

"You're Billy Sampson!" the girl said. "You're really Billy Sampson!"

"You're the girl who came to our dressing room before the show," Emma accused her.

"What's this all about? What were you doing in the van?" Billy demanded.

"Can we go inside?" Tina asked. "Because I'm really freezing out here."

"Do I know you?" Billy asked.

"No," Tina said excitedly, "but I'm so thrilled that I'm going to meet the whole band and—"

"How'd you get into the van?" Billy asked, sounding very irritated.

"You left the back door unlocked," Tina

said. "Not smart—even in Vermont. You never know who might drop in." This comment got a laugh from Becky and Allie. Billy looked at them sharply.

"Maybe we should go in," Emma said, a resigned tone in her voice. She turned and led the way to the front door. The others followed behind her.

Kurt was right behind her, as he was the first person out of the other cars. He shook the snow off his boots and followed Emma to the kitchen, where she intended to do a quick inventory of the refrigerator and the cupboard.

"Who's the kid?" he asked softly, his voice full of concern. "And where'd she come from?"

Emma sighed and took Kurt by the arm. "I'm not sure," she said. "I know her name is Tina. She says she drove up with some friends from Brenford, New Hampshire, to see the show, but we think she hitchhiked here by herself. She saw the Flirts on that big tour we did, I guess. She's a fan."

"You *know* her?" Kurt asked.

"Not really," Emma said. "But she came to our dressing room to meet the band before the show."

"Do you think her parents know she's here?" Kurt asked.

"I doubt it."

"Well," Kurt said, "I'm going to find out."

Emma nodded agreement. Together, she and Kurt walked into the living room, where Tina had quickly ensconced herself in front of the fireplace and was busily building a fire. Everyone else was shaking snow out of their clothes or lining up to use one of the bathrooms.

"Tina?" Emma said to the girl. "I'm Emma Cresswell, one of the backup singers."

"I remember you from backstage," Tina said, her voice friendly.

"Tina, do you have a last name?" Emma asked.

"Just call me Tina," the girl said.

"Tina, do your parents know you're in Vermont?" Emma asked, sitting down beside the thin girl.

Tina shrugged and poked some more twigs into the fire. "I told them I was coming with, um, my cousin."

"I thought you said you drove up with friends," Emma reminded her, recalling Tina and Sam's conversation in the doorway of the dressing room.

"Oh, yeah. Well, I did," Tina said.

"So where are they?" Kurt asked.

"Who?" Tina replied.

"Your friends," Kurt said patiently.

"What friends?" Tina asked blankly.

"The friends you just said you rode up here with," Kurt said with exasperation.

"I didn't—" Tina began.

"Just a minute," Emma interrupted. She took a deep breath. "Look, Tina, we're only trying to help. Now, I heard you say you drove up with some friends."

"I guess I did say that," Tina admitted.

"So?" Emma asked. "Is it true?"

"I said it," Tina said slowly, "but . . . well, there aren't any friends."

"And your cousin?"

Tina shook her head. "Basically, I kind of lied."

"You lied."

"Yeah," Tina admitted. "I figured you'd get all bent out of shape if I told you that I hitched a ride up by myself. I am just so sorry."

Emma sighed for about the fifth time since she'd gotten back to the house.

"We've got to call your parents," Kurt said authoritatively. "What's their number?"

Tina turned toward the fire, which was now blazing. She added a log to the pile of burning twigs. She didn't answer.

"I asked you, Tina, what's their number?" Kurt repeated.

"And I'm telling you, whatever your name is, that I'm not telling you!" Tina said forcefully.

Emma put her hand on the girl's arm. "You have to tell us," she insisted.

"Why?" the girl asked. "They don't care about me."

"I'm sure that's not true," Emma said.

"You don't know," Tina said. "Do you think every kid has parents who care

103

about her? That's a stupid sitcom fantasy."

"Are you saying there isn't anyone who cares about where you are? Or if you're okay?" Emma pressed.

Tina shrugged.

"Look, just give me your home phone number," Kurt said firmly. "I mean it."

"Why?" Tina said again.

"Because—" Emma began.

"Because if you don't," Kurt interrupted softly, sitting down next to the teen, "I'm going to have to call the state police."

Tina looked at him. "You wouldn't do that," she said quickly. "I'm a rocker, like you guys! You wouldn't turn me in. You couldn't!"

I can't believe this is happening, Emma thought as Kurt gave Tina a hard look. *Not only do I have Diana and her cousin here, plus Becky and Allie, but I also have to deal with an enormous blizzard and a runaway kid.*

"Don't push me, Tina," Kurt said. "I'm giving you one more chance."

Tina gave Kurt a smirk in response.

"It's your decision," Kurt said finally, getting up and going over to the phone. "You want to give me your parents' number now?"

Tina stared at the fire, pointedly ignoring Kurt, who stood by the phone, staring at her.

Kurt picked up the phone and put it to his ear.

"Damn," he said. "Damn, damn, damn."

"What is it?" Emma asked, getting to her feet.

"Phone's dead," Kurt reported.

"It's dead?" Tina echoed happily.

"You're joking," Emma replied.

He handed Emma the receiver, and she listened for a dial tone.

There wasn't one.

"Unbelievable," she said softly.

"Guess you won't be calling anyone," Tina said smugly, playing with a twig from the kindling basket next to the fireplace.

"The snow must have knocked down

the phone lines," Kurt said. "They could be down for a while."

"What are we going to do?" Emma asked.

"You're gonna deal with me," Tina offered, from her place by the fire. "Whether you like it or not."

Thank goodness the power is still on, Emma thought as she stood in the kitchen, popping yet another huge batch of popcorn for her houseguests. *I remember the last time I was in a power blackout—it was in New York with Sam and Carrie when Sam was rehearsing for that Broadway show. Somehow I think a blackout up here would be a lot cozier. Or maybe it would be scarier. I'm not sure which!*

It was nearly two o'clock in the morning, but just about everyone was still awake. Between the gig and the snowstorm, there'd been too much excitement for anyone to go to sleep.

And still the snow came down—there seemed to be no sign that it was relenting. According to the news, they were in for a lot more snow. It was going to be one of the biggest blizzards the Northeast had ever seen.

Emma poured the popcorn into a bowl and carried it back into the living room. Some of her friends were gathered around the television, watching it avidly.

"Hey, they're skiing in New York City," Jay said, pointing at the television.

"Is the phone still out?" Kurt asked, making a gesture with his chin toward Tina. She was fast asleep on the floor, covered by a blanket that Emma had pulled out for her.

"It was when I last checked," Emma reported.

"I'd entertain us," Pres drawled, "if I could get this person out of my lap." He looked down at Sam, who was lying with her head comfortably in Pres's lap.

"You wish," Sam said, her eyes closed. But when Pres started tickling her, she sat up in a hurry.

"Quit it!" she cried, but Pres wouldn't

stop. "C'mon, cut it out, or I'll sic Dee Dee on you. . . . Hey, where is Dee Dee, anyway?"

"She and Diana are asleep in the back," Emma said.

"Thank God," Allie Jacobs quipped.

"Double thank God," Becky added.

"You interested in some musical entertainment?" Pres asked.

"Sure," Carrie said from her spot on the couch where she was snuggled next to Billy.

"Snowstorm serenade," Pres joked, getting up and going over to get his guitar. Then he flipped the lights off. Suddenly the room was illuminated solely by the red glow of the fire.

"Nice," Kurt said, nuzzling Emma, who had sat down next to him on the couch. "I like it."

Emma tried to smile. *I think it's romantic, too,* she thought, *but I'm too tired even to think about romance. And the idea of taking care of all these people here isn't exactly romantic, either!*

Pres played a couple of tentative chords on the acoustic guitar as he figured out what he was going to play.

Then he started to finger-pick a couple of slow, bluesy riffs. His deep, warm baritone voice took over the melody, and he started in on an old spiritual that Emma and her friends had sung many times before.

Sometimes I feel like a motherless child,
Sometimes I feel like a motherless child,
Sometimes I feel like a motherless child,
A long, long, long, long way from home.

That's my song, Emma recalled. *That's the one I used to audition for the Flirts. I love that song.*

"This one's for the kid," Pres said softly. "It's for Tina."

Sometimes I feel like a motherless child.
Sometimes I feel like a motherless child.
Sometimes I feel like a motherless child.
A long, long, long, long way from home.

Sometimes I feel like I'm old and gone.
Sometimes I feel like I'm old and gone.
Soemtimes I feel like I'm old and gone,
A long, long, long, long way from home.

"That kid's sufferin'," Pres said, his fingers still picking the guitar strings. He gave Emma and Kurt a quick look. "Don't forget it."

And then he sang the chorus one more time.

Sometimes I feel like a motherless child.
A long, long, long, long way from home.

Emma couldn't help it. Her clear soprano joined in on the last two lines. And when the song was done, everyone in the room nodded. Pres had said more with his song than they could have in a year of talking.

Emma looked over at Tina, at her pale little face, at her fingernails, which were bitten down to the quick. *Who are you?* she thought. *What made you so unhappy that you would run away from home at Christmas time?*

Tina stirred in her sleep and rolled over. She settled into a more comfortable position, and began to snore very lightly.

Tina is suffering, Emma thought. *And I can't forget that. Or how lucky I am to have all the friends I do have.*

EIGHT

"I've never seen this much snow in my life," Emma said as she peered out of the picture window in the living room.

It was the next morning, and it still had not stopped snowing. If anything, it was snowing even harder.

Emma turned to Carrie, who stood next to her, staring out at the snow. "Did you hear the weather report?"

Carrie nodded. "It's not supposed to let up until at least this afternoon," she said with a sigh.

Sam came up beside her. "The twins and Dee Dee are screaming at each other in the kitchen," she reported.

"What's it about this time?" Carrie asked with a sigh.

"Something about some guy on some TV show, if you can believe that," Sam said. "Becky said this guy was cute, and Dee Dee said she had gone out with him when she was on vacation in Los Angeles, and Allie called Dee Dee a liar, and Dee Dee called the twins fat, ugly pig-oinkers who couldn't get a cute guy if their lives depended on it."

"Lovely," Emma said.

"Listen, I don't recall deciding to include any of the junior set when we planned this trip, do you?" Sam asked.

"There's no privacy at all," Carrie moaned.

"Tell me about it," Sam agreed, still staring out at the snow. "Pres went to kiss me last night and I heard this voice behind me saying, 'He could do so much better!'"

"Diana?" Carrie asked.

"Dee Dee," Sam reported. "Diana's been almost civil, which is really weird."

"No, it isn't," Emma said.

Sam turned to look at her. "Please tell me you're not defending Diana De Witt."

"I'm not," Emma said. "I just know what she's up to. She wants to be back in the band."

"I know she does," someone whispered from behind them.

All three of them turned around. It was Erin, whose voice had improved only marginally.

"She's no threat to you," Emma assured Erin.

"Are you sure?" Erin rasped.

"Are you kidding?" Sam asked. "None of us can stand her!"

"She's cute," Erin whispered.

"If you mean she's thin, well, yeah, she's thin," Sam admitted. "But you're just as good-looking. Better-looking!"

Emma smiled at Sam. *She's come so far,* Emma thought. *I'm really proud of her.*

"And you sing much better than she does," Carrie added.

"Thanks," Erin whispered. "I just feel so bad that I couldn't do the gig with you guys. . . ." Erin's voice sounded as if it was about to give out completely.

"Hey, you'd better save what voice you've got," Sam suggested. "Go back to writing everything down."

"You guys," Tina called, running into the living room. "Billy says to come into the kitchen and listen to the radio."

"Why, are they playing a Flirts tune?" Sam asked.

"Road conditions or something," Tina said with a shrug.

They all hurried into the kitchen, where Billy, Pres, Jay, and Jake were huddled around the radio.

"What's up?" Sam asked.

"Shh!" Billy hissed, leaning closer to the radio.

". . . To repeat this update, heavy snow has caused an avalanche, completely closing Route 7 and the Croachee Bridge Road. Two cars are believed to have been buried in the avalanche. Casualty figures are not yet available. These roads are closed until further notice. Police estimate that it will be at least two days before the roads will reopen."

Carrie paled. "Those poor people . . ."

"Route 7 and the Croachee Bridge Road is the only way out of here," Emma said.

"Are you sure?" Jake asked.

"Positive," Emma said. "I know this area really well."

Everyone just stood there looking at everyone else for a minute.

"Well, I guess that means we're all staying here for a while," Kurt finally said.

"I'm starving," Diana said, sailing into the kitchen. "Who's making breakfast?" She stopped in her tracks. "Did someone die or something?"

"We're snowed in," Pres explained, clicking off the radio.

"We can't be snowed in," Diana said. "I've got to catch a plane. Dee Dee and I are going to Hawaii. Her parents and my parents are already there."

Carrie shrugged. "The road is closed. There was an avalanche."

"Too cool!" Tina cried.

"It's not cool, you little idiot," Diana spat out. "How am I supposed to get to Hawaii?"

"Get on your broom and fly," Sam suggested under her breath.

"Look, there's nothing we can do but listen to the reports and wait it out," Emma said. "I'll make some breakfast for everyone."

"I'll have two egg whites and dry toast," Diana ordered.

"I'll have what she's having," Dee Dee echoed, coming into the kitchen.

"Hey, this isn't a restaurant, you know," Becky said, sidling up beside Dee Dee.

"We have only a few eggs left," Emma explained, "and I was saving them to make Christmas cookies." She looked around at the huge group. "I . . . well, I mean, we didn't plan on food for so many people."

"We'll just have to ration the food," Kurt said. He reached for Emma's hand. "How about if everyone clears out of the kitchen, and Emma and I will figure something out for breakfast, okay?"

"Can I stay and help?" Tina asked in a small voice.

"Sure," Kurt said. "We'll call the rest of you when breakfast is ready."

"Hey, I found a Monopoly set in that closet in the hall," Becky said. "Let's go play!"

"You'd probably cheat," Dee Dee said as she followed Becky and the others out of the kitchen.

"Wow," Emma said, shaking her head. "Snowed in . . . pretty unbelievable, huh?"

"Yeah," Kurt agreed. "Do we have enough food here for this crew?"

"I certainly didn't think we'd have this many people," Emma said with concern. "And we can't even get to the store."

"There's some oatmeal," Tina reported, opening a large cupboard. "And let's see what else . . . A large box of prunes."

Kurt chuckled. "Oatmeal and prunes, yum."

Emma opened the refrigerator. "Okay, we've got some frozen pizzas that we can

119

use for dinner tonight—but everyone is going to be limited to one and a half pieces. For lunch tomorrow we can make sandwiches—"

"Are we limited to one and a half sandwiches?" Kurt teased.

"I'm serious," Emma said, still staring into the refrigerator. "We don't know when the road will be clear, and we've got to feed everybody."

"We could let Dee Dee starve," Tina said. "That would be fine with me."

"Has she been nasty to you, too?" Emma asked as she filled a pot with water for the oatmeal.

"Well, let's see," Tina said, leaning against the kitchen counter. "She told me I have buck teeth and I'd better get braces before people start to call me horse-face. She said my shirt is ugly. And she called me stupid. But then she told me she was only kidding."

"She always does that," Emma said. "Try to ignore her."

Tina shrugged. "She's probably right. I

probably am all those things." She reached into the cupboard and got out some bowls, which she set on the counter. Then she began to take silverware out of the drawer.

Emma sneaked a look at Kurt, then turned to Tina. "It doesn't sound as if you have a very high opinion of yourself."

"Hey, the truth is the truth, you know?" Tina said as she pulled a bunch of napkins from the package. "So, what's it like being perfect-looking and singing with the Flirts?"

"I'm hardly perfect-looking," Emma protested.

"Yeah, yeah. Perfect girls always say things like that," Tina said.

"I happen to think you're really cute," Kurt told Tina.

"Dream on," she snorted.

"I'm serious," Kurt said. "You have a very pretty face. Your hair is kind of messed up . . ."

"Who cares?" Tina shot back. "Who gets to decide what's pretty and what's ugly, anyway? My mom is always trying to get me to wear all this pastel, frilly crap—"

"Is that why you ran away?" Kurt interrupted.

"No," Tina said in a low voice.

"So why, then?" Kurt asked.

Tina folded her arms. "You'd never understand in a million years."

Emma poured oatmeal into the water boiling on the stove. "We might understand," she said, "if you gave us a chance."

Tina sighed. After a moment she said, "I'm like this pawn, okay?"

"What do you mean?" Emma asked, stirring the oatmeal. She turned the heat down underneath the pot.

Tina stared out the window. "Love is so stupid, don't you think?"

No one said anything.

"I mean, it's so fake," Tina went on. "My parents were married for, like, twenty years. And they were always so lovey-dovey—hugging and kissing and all that. My friends used to say I was so lucky because my parents were actually still married to each other and loved each other. . . ."

"Go on," Emma urged quietly.

"So last year my mom finds out my dad has been having this affair with his secretary, Felicia, for the past five years. Is that lame or what? All the time he's playing the dutiful husband and the perfect dad, he's bopping this bimbo who wears purple eye shadow and spike heels!"

"That stinks," Kurt said in a low voice.

"Tell me about it," Tina agreed. "So my dad moves out, right? But he wants to spend all this time with me. And he tells me the only reason he started this big affair with Felicia was because my mother never made him feel like a 'real man'— whatever that means. So I go home to Mom, and she starts telling me how all the Christmas gifts that Dad gave me every year were never really from him, that he was too busy to even think about me, that she picked them out and wrote out a card and signed his name."

"Now I see," Emma said. "Each of them

is blaming the other one, and you're stuck in the middle."

"I just don't want to hear what they have to say anymore," Tina said, tears coming to her eyes. She quickly wiped them away with the sleeve of her flannel shirt. "All the lovey-dovey stuff was just so much crap. That's all it was. Crap."

"Love is real," Emma said. "At least I think it is."

"Good for you," Tina said sarcastically.

Emma turned the heat off under the oatmeal. "Your parents are wrong to put you in the middle."

"Big duh," Tina replied.

"I'm sure they love you," Emma said. "They're just hurting right now."

"Maybe you need to tell them how you feel," Kurt suggested.

"Yeah, like they care," Tina said. "I told you you wouldn't understand, so let's just drop it, okay?" She turned and marched out of the kitchen.

"Well, we really blew that, didn't we?" Emma said.

"A lot of kids have it a lot worse than Tina," Kurt said.

"That doesn't make her pain any less real," Emma said gently. *Just like having millions didn't make my relationship with Kat any better,* she thought. *I still don't know what to say to her, any more than Tina seems to know what to say to her parents.*

So how can I help her when I can't even help myself?

> The water is wide
> I can not get o'er
> And neither have I
> Wings to fly.
> Give me a boat
> That can carry two
> And both shall row
> My love and I . . .

Carrie closed her eyes and listened as Billy sang the sweet, sad words of the old folk song "The Water Is Wide," accompanying himself with a few simple chords on his acoustic guitar.

I could listen to him sing to me forever, she thought happily. *His voice is so beautiful.* . . .

> I lean my back
> Up against an oak
> I thought it was
> A trusty tree
> But first it swayed
> And then it broke
> And so my false love
> Did unto me.

Carrie opened her eyes and looked around the living room, lit only by the fire roaring in the huge stone fireplace. They had eaten pizza and bowls of popcorn for dinner, and now everyone was in the living room, listening to Billy play the guitar.

The snow had finally stopped. According to the radio, it had been a record three-foot snowfall, with drifts up to six feet. Now the wind was howling, blowing the snow against the picture window. The main roads were still closed, and the roads that had been blocked by the avalanche would be closed for at least another two days. The phone was still out.

I suppose we should be glad that we still have electricity and heat, Carrie thought as she listened to Billy sing the final, poignant notes of the song. *But I just don't know how we're going to make the food stretch if we're stuck here for too long.*

"Wow, that was beautiful," Tina said when Billy had finished. "You're better than Kurt Cobain, no lie."

"And unlike Cobain, he's smart enough not to off himself," Sam put in.

"Thanks," Billy said with a grin.

"Tina's right, you know," Diana said, giving Billy a sexy look from her spot on the rug in front of the fire.

"Thanks," Billy said again.

"You know, Billy, you've really inspired me," Diana continued.

Sam, who was sitting on the couch with her head on Pres's shoulder, put her finger down her throat. "Gag me, Diana."

Diana shot her a cool glance. "I'm sorry if you have such a juvenile reaction to a sincere compliment."

"You don't really expect me to fall for that, do you?" Sam said.

"Sam, I'm a professional musician," Diana said. "I take music very seriously."

"God, get me the hurl sack!" Sam exclaimed.

"Me too," Becky agreed.

"Me too," Allie said.

"Why don't the three of you just grow up?" Dee Dee snapped.

"Hey, can we all just chill out?" Pres drawled.

"What a good idea," Diana said smoothly. She sat up and stretched ostentatiously, her tight black bodysuit straining across her chest. She put her hand on her stomach. "I can't believe I ate pizza for dinner. It's so fattening!"

"You only ate a piece and a half," Tina pointed out. "That's all any of us ate."

Diana looked over at Erin, who was sitting on the rug, her back against the couch, holding hands with Jake. "I guess it was hard on you, Erin, not getting more to eat."

"I'm fine," Erin whispered, her face growing red with embarrassment.

"Oh, good," Diana said. "I just meant that I'm sure you're used to eating a lot more than that."

"Play something else," Emma told Billy, eager to change the subject.

"Actually, I have something to play," Diana said.

"You don't play the guitar," Jay reminded her.

"I know that," Diana said, reaching into her back pocket. "But I wrote this song—I told you that you inspired me, Billy—and the guitar chords are right there under the lyrics." She handed the sheet of paper to Billy.

"Wow, I suddenly have to change rooms," Sam said, jumping up from the couch.

"Bye-bye," Dee Dee said.

Sam paused in the doorway and said, "No one wants to hear your stupid little song, Diana."

"Speak for your stupid little self," Dee Dee shot back.

"This is really silly," Emma said.

"Yeah," Kurt agreed, giving Sam a significant look. "If we're all stuck here together, we might as well be civil to each other."

"Easy for you to say," Dee Dee pouted. "Diana was the one who wanted to be here. *I* was supposed to be in Hawaii!"

"No one cares, Dee Dee," Becky sang out.

"Just shut up," Dee Dee snapped.

"You shut up!" Becky shot back.

"So, do you want to try my song?" Diana asked, ignoring the argument.

"I'm out of here," Sam said, heading toward the stairs.

"Excuse me, y'all," Pres said, and followed Sam.

"Carrie and I are going to take a walk

in the snow," Billy said, putting his guitar down.

"We're coming, too," Kurt said, pulling Emma up with him.

"Oh, so that's how it is," Diana said in a steely voice. "I help you guys out of your jam because fatso over there can't sing, and this is how you treat me!"

"You know, Diana, you make me kind of sick," Jake said, as he helped Erin up. "Erin is more beautiful than you are any day of the week, inside and out." The two of them walked out of the room. Jay shook his head and followed them. Which left Diana with Dee Dee, Tina, Becky, and Allie.

The twins immediately began to ignore Dee Dee and turned their attention to Diana.

"Ha!" Becky yelped with glee. "No one fell for it, Diana. We know you're trying to get back into the Flirts."

"And it isn't going to work," Allie added.

"I'll listen to your song, Diana," Dee Dee offered.

"Oh, just shut up," Diana barked. "This is the worst Christmas of my entire life."

Then she tore the lyrics of her song into a dozen tiny pieces and threw them into the fire.

NINE

"Let's see," Carrie mused, looking into the cupboard late the next day. "It looks like we've got just enough stuff to make a batch of Christmas cookies."

"Better make it a huge batch," Diana said as she sipped a cup of hot chocolate at the kitchen table. "Erin will eat enough for two."

"How do you even live with yourself?" Carrie asked her pointedly.

"Carrie, please tell Dee Dee to shut up. She's driving us crazy," Becky said, coming into the kitchen.

"She says the Zit People is the worst band she's ever heard," Allie said. "She said Ian is a short, ugly little turd."

"The truth hurts, I suppose," Dee Dee said as she plopped down next to Diana at the table.

"Aren't you going to say you were just kidding?" Becky asked Dee Dee in a voice dripping with venom.

"No," Dee Dee replied, "because I wasn't." Tina was sitting across from her, polishing her fingernails with black nail polish. "I suppose you think that looks good," Dee Dee said.

"Better than your face," Tina replied, dipping the brush back into the polish.

"Oh, I'm soooo hurt," Dee Dee groaned, pressing her hand to her heart theatrically.

It was only three o'clock in the afternoon, and already everyone seemed to be bickering with everyone else. Diana seemed to hold the others personally responsible for the snowstorm and the fact that she was missing her trip to Hawaii. Dee Dee delighted in tormenting the twins and Tina. The twins were now wearing Sam's clothes, since they didn't have extra clothes with them. Sam wasn't too thrilled with that, and she kept complaining that there wasn't enough food and she was starving. Diana and Emma had had a major fight when Diana began to flirt with Kurt, at which point Kurt told Diana off and she went stomping off to her room. Billy kept obsessing about Cody Leete and whether or not the Flirts were ever going to get into the studio. Carrie thought she might be coming down with Erin's cold. And the only reason Erin wasn't involved was because she still didn't have much of her voice back.

"So, what about it?" Carrie asked, determined to stay cheerful. "Everyone up for Christmas cookies?"

"Hanukkah cookies," Becky Jacobs corrected Carrie, folding her arms. "Tonight is the first night of Hanukkah, you know."

"What's the difference?" Tina asked as she painted the nail of her pinky.

"One is Christian and one is Jewish, stupid," Dee Dee said.

Tina looked at Becky. "Are you Jewish?"

"Uh-huh," Becky said. "My dad must

135

be having a fit that we're not home." She turned to her sister. "You think he's called the police by now?"

"I'm surprised he hasn't hired a pilot to fly a plane out here and rescue us," Allie said.

"He'd have to have figured out where we are to do that," Becky pointed out.

"Well, he's smart," Allie said. "I'm sure he's figured it out. Besides, he's used to having Sam look out for us."

Becky ran her palm over the kitchen counter. "We've never had Hanukkah without Dad before."

"You guys are really Jewish?" Tina asked again, wide-eyed.

"We just said that," Allie pointed out. "What is the biggie?"

Tina shrugged. "I never knew anyone Jewish before, that's all."

"Where have you been living, under a rock?" Dee Dee asked.

Tina shrugged again. "I live in a real small town. There aren't any Jewish kids at my school." She looked at the twins. "So, what's it like to be Jewish?"

"Cool," Becky replied.

"Cool," Allie echoed.

Sam came into the kitchen. "You guys, I am *starving*," she said, opening the door to the refrigerator. "There's got to be something I can eat."

"Sam's Jewish, too," Allie told Tina.

"For real?" Tina asked.

"Sorta," Sam said, her head still buried inside the refrigerator. "How about this piece of cheese?" she asked. "I can eat that, can't I?"

"I'm using it to make lunch," Carrie said.

"Bummer," Sam said, closing the fridge. "I'm gonna completely starve to death before they get that stupid road open."

"What's it like to be Jewish?" Tina asked Sam.

"Confusing," Sam replied.

"How come?"

"Well, see, I'm Jewish . . . but I'm not Jewish," Sam began. "It's kind of hard to explain."

"Can I tell her?" Becky asked.

"It's okay with me," Sam said with a

137

shrug. She boosted herself up to the kitchen counter and sat there, her long legs dangling.

"Sam is adopted," Becky explained. "And she was raised Christian. But her birth parents are Jewish."

"So, which are you," Dee Dee asked Sam. "Jewish or Christian?"

"Both, I guess," Sam said.

"You can't be both," Allie pointed out. "It isn't logical."

"Since when am I logical?" Sam asked.

"Tonight is the first night of Hanukkah," Becky said wistfully. "We don't even have a menorah."

"What's that?" Tina asked.

"This special candleholder for Hanukkah," Allie said. "A candle is lit on each of the eight nights of Hanukkah."

"We get presents every night for eight nights," Becky added.

"Cool!" Tina exclaimed. "So it's like a long Christmas, right?"

"Hanukkah is the Festival of Lights," Allie said. "See, back in ancient times there was this big fight between the Jews and the Syrians, because the Syrians didn't want to let the Jews practice their faith."

"They weren't the last," Carrie said wryly.

"Anyway," Allie continued, "the Jews won and got to relight this sacred lamp in their Temple, which the Syrians had ruined. That's what the holiday's about."

"I never knew that," Tina mused.

"Neither did I," Sam admitted.

"It's not a very important holiday in our religion. There are others that mean more," Becky explained. "That's what Dad says, anyway. But in America Hanukkah's turned into, like, this Christmas thing— you know, presents and everything."

"Wow, I feel so sorry for you," Tina said sincerely. "You don't get to celebrate Christmas!"

"We don't care," Allie said. "I mean, you don't get to celebrate Hanukkah, or Purim, or Passover."

"What's all that?" Tina asked.

"Those are all these really cool Jewish holidays—" Allie began.

"Yeah," Tina interrupted, "but still, no Christmas . . . I can't even imagine it!"

I know what she means, Sam thought. *I can't imagine it, either. But if I'd never been adopted, I never would have celebrated Christmas. What would that be like? I mean, Christmas is such a big deal! The whole country goes Christmas-crazy for two months. It's Christmas this and Christmas that, Christmas songs and everything green and red, and everyone saying Merry Christmas to each other.*

What if you say Merry Christmas to someone who doesn't celebrate Christmas? How would they feel?

How would I feel?

"Anyhow, I think it sounds pretty interesting," Tina decided, blowing on her newly applied black nail polish. "So, Merry Hanukkah!"

"*Happy* Hanukkah, you moron," Dee Dee corrected her.

"Why do you always call everyone names?" Becky asked, turning on Dee Dee. "What is your problem?"

"I was just trying to explain—" Dee Dee began.

"How about if we just all say 'happy holidays'?" Carrie suggested. "That covers everything."

"Including New Year's!" Allie added with a grin, and everyone smiled.

"Well, happy holidays, then," Tina said.

"Thanks," Becky said.

"But what about that thing you guys were talking about before?" Tina asked.

"What thing?" Allie queried.

Tina held out her hands, as if she were holding something in them. "That medorah thing," she said.

"Menorah," Allie corrected.

"Whatever," Tina said.

Becky shrugged. "We don't have one here."

"We have this really cool one at home," Allie said wistfully. "Mom's mom brought it back from Israel when we were just little babies. . . ."

"I heard some things about your mom," Dee Dee said knowingly.

This is a very dangerous topic of con-

versation, Carrie thought. *The twins' mom ran out on the family years ago, and no one even knows where she is.* "Who wants to help me bake cookies?" she said, trying to distract the younger girls.

"You shut up about our mother," Becky told Dee Dee in a threatening voice. "I mean it."

Dee Dee just raised her eyebrows and didn't say a word.

"So, can you guys celebrate Hanukkah without one of those menorah things?" Tina asked.

"I guess we'll have to," Allie said. "Because of the storm."

Tina nodded.

"I'm sure of one thing, though," Allie added.

"What's that?" Tina asked.

"God will understand if we don't have one," Allie said. "I'm sure He'll understand."

"Or She'll understand," Becky said with a grin.

"He *or* She? Now *that* is really stupid," Dee Dee said.

"No, it isn't," Becky insisted. "My Hebrew teacher told me that God has both male and female characteristics."

"And there's no word that combines both," Allie concluded.

What about me? Sam thought. *What about me? Am I supposed to celebrate Christmas? Or Hanukkah? Or both? And will He-She understand how confused I am about it?*

"Pssst!"

"Hey, Sam, wake up!" Allie whispered gently.

Sam, who had been taking a quick nap in her bedroom, woke up to see Becky and Allie hovering over her.

"What time is it?" Sam asked groggily, pulling herself to a sitting position. She'd been asleep for about an hour or so.

"About five o'clock, you sleepyhead," Becky reported. "Get up, come on!"

"Did the road get opened?" Sam asked, her stomach growling slightly. "Is there food now?"

"You wish," Allie said. "We're going to

be having wet newspapers for dinner at this rate."

"How long can a human live without food? That's what I want to know," Sam moaned.

"We did eat lunch," Becky reminded her. "We had—"

"Half a sandwich each," Sam put in. "That is not my concept of lunch. Now let me go back to sleep and dream about food. Right now I want it more than I want Pres."

She turned over, but Becky grabbed her arm and yanked her to a sitting position. "Come with us," she said. "Come on!"

"Okay, okay," Sam said. "Quit pulling on me!" At that moment she realized what Becky was wearing. "Hey, that's my sweater you have on!"

"Well, you said we could wear your clothes," Becky reminded her.

"I said you could wear what I gave you to wear," Sam said, "not anything you wanted!"

"Forget that now," Allie sad. "We have to hurry!"

Sam got up—she'd fallen asleep still wearing her clothes—and followed Becky and Allie out of the bedroom and into the small breakfast nook off the kitchen. For once there was no one in the kitchen—not that there was much food for anyone to cook.

"So, what do you think?" Allie asked, her voice proud.

"Of what?" Sam asked, puzzled. All she saw was on old box upside down on the table.

"*Ta-da!*" Allie cried. She and Becky lifted the box off the table. Under it, gleaming white in the warm light of the kitchen, was a small snow and branch sculpture resting in a lasagna pan. It had a stocky base, and an elongated top, with eight small holes punched in the top. One of the holes was on a pedestal that was slightly taller than the others.

"A menorah," Becky pronounced. "We'd better light it fast."

"Before it melts," Allie added.

Sam stood before it, speechless. She was astonished by the twins' resourcefulness.

"You girls are unbelievable," she finally exclaimed.

"True." Allie grinned as Becky reached down and picked up two birthday candles that were lying in the lasagna dish.

"It's the best we could do," Becky explained, popping one of the candles into the middle of the menorah and the other into the end of one of the branches.

Sam looked on, enraptured by this simple ritual.

"So," Allie said, "who's going to do the blessing?"

"Hey, y'all," Pres's voice drawled from the doorway, "what's going on in there?"

"Nothing," Allie called back.

"You can't fool me, Allie Jacobs," Pres said as he made his way into the kitchen and stood by Sam's side. "What have we here?"

"It's a Hanukkah menorah," Becky said.

"Eight nights. A candle each night, right?" Pres said.

"Right!" Becky said, her eyes shining. "How do you know that?"

"Yeah, big guy," Sam said, smiling up into her boyfriend's warm eyes, "how do you know that—being from Tennessee and all?"

"I've been around," Pres answered. "Actually, I learned about it in Sunday school at our church when I was a kid."

"No way," Becky said.

"Way," Pres replied, his grin growing wider. "So what are y'all doin' in here with this?"

"It's Hanukkah," Allie explained. "We're lighting—"

"No, that's not what I mean. I said, what are you doing in *here* with it? Just bring it into the living room and light it there," Pres insisted.

"But—"

"Come on," Pres said. "We're gonna celebrate Christmas out there. Why shouldn't you celebrate Hanukkah there, too?"

And without waiting for Allie or Becky to agree, he picked up the lasagna dish and carried the menorah with him out of the kitchen and into the living room.

Almost everyone was in the living room, except for Diana and Dee Dee, who were off playing a Nintendo game together in another room.

"Time to light the menorah," Pres told the gathered group.

"Far out," Tina said with a grin.

"Everyone know what Hanukkah is about?" Pres queried. The whole group nodded.

"So, Becky and Allie," Pres instructed, setting the snow menorah down on the coffee table, "take it away."

Pres went over and flipped off the light switch at exactly the same time that Becky struck a match to light the candles.

"Blessed art Thou, O Lord, ruler of the universe, who has bidden us to kindle the Hanukkah lights," Becky said, touching the match to the top candle.

Sam could see how her face beamed with happiness in the reflected candlelight, and she herself was filled with a warm feeling that she didn't recognize.

I'm a part of this, she realized. *This is my menorah. This is my holiday, too—I think.*

"Blessed art Thou, O Lord," Becky continued, "ruler—"

"What's that?" Kurt exclaimed.

"Shh!" Sam shushed him.

"No, listen!" Kurt said.

The group in the living room all fell silent and strained their ears.

Kurt was right. There was a sound like a chain saw or an airplane, coming from outside.

"It's the National Guard," Sam quipped, "dropping us supplies by parachute. Please, I need junk food!"

"Quiet!" Kurt said.

The sound got louder and louder, until it was almost deafening—it clearly was an airplane, probably a small one. And judging from the sporadic sputtering of the engine, this was an airplane in trouble.

"Come on!" Kurt shouted. He ran outside, and everyone tumbled after him, the menorah temporarily forgotten.

And there, from the front porch of the

house, Emma, Sam and Carrie saw something that they would never forget for the rest of their lives.

In the bright light of the full moon they watched as a small single-engine airplane seemed to stop in midair, and then slowly, ever so slowly, plummet to the ground.

TEN

"Oh my God," Sam screamed.

Just off to their right, on the lakeshore, a plane had crashed. They could see the wreckage smoking in the moonlight, though the fuselage was too far away from them to be seen clearly.

"Hey, did someone just scream?" Dee Dee asked, running onto the porch, Diana at her side.

"A . . . a plane just crashed," Emma managed to say. She pointed.

"Wow," Diana breathed.

"Come on!" Kurt finally cried. "We've got to help them! Hurry! Hurry!"

"What should we do?" Emma asked.

"Follow me, all of you!" Kurt yelled.

"We have to put on coats first," Carrie said practically, running toward the hall closet.

"Grab my coat and Kurt's," Billy told Carrie.

Everyone quickly scrambled into their winter gear while Kurt and Billy ran down the short staircase from the porch to the snow-covered yard. Emma picked up the first-aid kit on her way out.

"Ouch!" Diana cried as her ankle turned on the icy steps.

"Are you okay?" Dee Dee asked her, grabbing her arm.

"Yeah. Let's just hurry," Diana said, hobbling a little.

But at the bottom of the stairs they stopped. They were confronted by a wall of snow four feet high.

"What are we doing to do?" Carrie cried, contemplating the snowdrift. She looked at Emma and Sam, who both had horrified looks on their faces.

"The cars have four-wheel drive," Emma remembered. "They might—"

"Never," Kurt said, shaking his head.

"They'd be bogged down in a New York minute," Pres agreed.

"Then what are we going to do?" Emma asked. "We can't just leave those people out there!"

"I know," Kurt said, lines of tension etched into his forehead.

"Maybe the snow is packed enough that we can walk on top of it," Becky suggested.

Billy shook his head. "I don't think so. It's too new. And it's not icy enough."

"But we have to *do* something!" Sam cried.

Emma grabbed Sam's hand and held it fast. *What if there are people on that plane bleeding to death?* Emma thought in a panic. *What if they're trapped in the wreckage? The roads are still blocked, and no one can get through to help us. The neighbors are a couple of miles away at the other end of the lake—too far to reach. What are we going to do?*

"Quick," Kurt commanded, making a

153

hurried decision. "Everyone inside. Put on more clothes. And boots."

"I don't have any boots here," Diana said. "I was on my way to Hawaii, remember?"

"Well, just do the best you can," Kurt yelled as he ran back up the stairs.

Everyone scrambled to follow Kurt's direction. The twins were dressed first and stood around waiting for everyone, practically jumping up and down with anxiety.

"We have to hurry!" Becky cried. "Someone could be dying out there!"

"Oh, God," Allie moaned, "I just thought of something. What if it's Dad? What if he *did* hire a pilot so he could come and find us?"

The twins turned to Emma and Kurt, who had just arrived on the porch, bundled in their warmest clothes.

"Please," Becky cried, grabbing Emma's hand, tears in her eyes, "it might be my dad out there!"

"We're gonna do everything we can,"

Kurt promised as he looked around the porch.

"What are you looking for?" Emma asked him, glancing anxiously at the still-smoking wreckage. It seemed to be smoking less now. *It never actually caught fire,* she thought. *That's good.*

"Got it!" Kurt exclaimed, lifting up the top of a wooden box and discovering three or four snow shovels. Just as he was pulling the snow shovels out of the box, everyone else came out onto the porch and stood around expectantly. Someone had even found Tina, Dee Dee, and Diana warm clothing to wear, but they still didn't have any boots.

"Okay, everyone," Kurt ordered, "start with the shovels. We're digging our way out to the plane."

Kurt led the way back down the stairs to the wall of snow confronting them. With a grim look on his face, he arranged them into a two-by-two line, and they wordlessly started shoveling snow furiously. Once one of them was exhausted—it was tiring, back-breaking work—he or she handed the shovel to the next person, who dug right in. Even Diana and Dee Dee shoveled without complaint.

Slowly, surely, they made their way out toward the lakeshore, with high walls of snow on either side of them.

"You want me to take over?" Pres asked Sam, who was breathing hard, sweat pouring down her face.

"I can last a little longer," Sam replied, grimly digging her shovel into the heavy snow. When she felt she couldn't lift the shovel one more time, she handed it to Emma. And when Emma was done, she handed it to Diana.

Diana dug into the snow as fiercely as anyone.

The group inched its way toward the wreckage. Fortunately, the snow was still fairly light and airy.

If this had happened tomorrow, after the snow had a chance to settle, we'd never get out there to them, Emma thought, gulping hard.

But if this had happened tomorrow, Route 7 would be open and we could get help. Now, we're really on our own. Completely.

"It's Daddy out there," Becky cried, tears rolling down her face. "I know it is. Please, we have to hurry!"

"We're going as fast as we can, honey," Sam told her in soothing voice. "But it's probably not your father. Don't worry."

"But what if it is and we're not fast enough?" Allie asked, her lip quivering with fear.

Finally, after what seemed like forever but probably wasn't more than forty-five minutes or so, the group neared the partially wrecked plane.

"Is there any danger of it exploding or anything?" Diana asked nervously.

No one answered her, because no one knew.

It doesn't seem to be too badly damaged, Emma thought.

"The snow cushioned the impact," Kurt said as he approached the cockpit. "Thank God."

"So there's a chance they're still alive?" Carrie said.

"I think so," Kurt said. "Who's the smallest person here?"

"Me!" Tina called out. "I am."

"Come here," Kurt commanded. "We're going to boost you up there. Tell us what you see."

Billy and Kurt each grabbed one of Tina's ankles and boosted the girl up so that she could see into the plane. Everyone stood around silently. Sam shot a quick look at Diana. It looked as though she was actually praying. Becky and Allie held hands, their faces white, their eyes closed.

"Two people!" Tina reported. "A man—"

"It's Daddy!" Becky whimpered.

"—and a boy," Tina added.

"A boy?" Allie repeated.

"The man has curly blond hair, it looks like," Tina reported.

"That's not Dad!" Becky said in relief. "It isn't him!"

"And there's a dog!" Tina cried. "A big brown dog!

"Can you tell if they're breathing?"

Kurt asked. "Are they bleeding? Do they look okay?"

"The dog's alive! It's alive!" Tina reported. "I see it moving!"

"The people," Kurt repeated, speaking insistently. "Are the people alive?"

Tina looked in for a long time. And when she spoke again, her voice was small.

"I don't know," she said.

"Well, are *they* moving?" Kurt insisted.

"No."

"Not at all?" Billy called up to her.

"No."

"Can you see . . . any blood or anything?" Pres asked, trying to sound gentle.

"I can't tell," Tina said.

"Boost Emma up," Kurt told Billy and Pres. "She knows some first aid."

"Me?" Emma asked, stunned.

"You do know first aid," Sam said. "You helped your dad that time. You took a course—"

"You're right," Emma said, nodding. "I'll do whatever I can."

"Just do your best," Kurt advised as they lowered Tina to the ground.

"Good luck," Diana said, staring hard at Emma.

"Thanks," Emma said. She picked up the first-aid kit and tucked it inside her jacket.

Kurt and Billy hoisted Emma up to the plane.

Emma grabbed hold of the cockpit door and gave the handle a twist.

It opened.

Please, God, she prayed, *please let these people be okay. It's the day before Christmas Eve. And it's Hanukkah, too. If ever it was the time for a miracle, this is it.*

Quickly she found a handhold and slithered into the cockpit. As she did, the big dog slid past her, jumped down to the ice below, and began whining and barking.

But Emma's attention wasn't on the dog. It was on the two people still in the plane. The man and the boy were both still strapped into their seats, motionless.

They're dead, Emma thought. *Their*

*plane crashed—how could they be alive?
Oh my God. I can't face this. I can't. I
can't!*

But then she thought of the dog. If the
dog survived, maybe the people did, too.
She looked more closely. The man's chest
was going up and down. And so was the
boy's.

"They're alive!" Emma screamed with
joy. "They're both alive!"

"What's going on in there?" Kurt called
up.

"They're unconscious," Emma yelled
down. "Both of them."

"Don't move them!" Billy called up.
"Just in case there's any injury to their
spinal cords, okay?"

"Okay!" Emma called back down.

"See if there are any smelling salts in
the first-aid kit," Kurt called.

But Emma had already anticipated
Kurt's suggestion, and had opened the
white box with a big red cross on top of it.
Frantically she started pulling things
out of the kit, trying to find smelling
salts.

There they are, Emma thought, spotting the ampules. *God, please let these work, please, please.*

She snapped one of the ampules open under the nose of the man. An ammonia smell filled the cabin.

He opened his eyes immediately.

"Wha . . . what?" he mumbled.

"Shh!" Emma tried to calm him. "It's okay, you're going to be all right."

"Huh?"

"It's okay," Emma murmured, "it's okay."

She maneuvered herself around in the cockpit over to the unconscious boy. She snapped another ampule of smelling salts open under his nose. And, just like the man, the boy opened his eyes.

"Thank God," the man said.

"Are you hurt?" Emma asked the man.

"I . . . I don't know."

"Please be careful," Emma warned him. "Do you have feeling in your arms?"

He nodded yes.

"And your legs?"

He nodded again.

"Can you wiggle your toes?" Emma asked.

"Yeah," he replied. He reached over and uncoupled his shoulder harness and seat belt.

"Is this your son?" Emma asked, looking at the boy, who appeared to be about the same age as Becky and Allie.

"Yes."

The boy looked up at Emma. "My arm hurts," he said in a small voice.

Emma ran her fingers up and down the arm. "Well," she told the boy and his father, "it might be broken, but it's not serious. For the time being, try not to move it too much."

"What's going on in there?" Kurt yelled up. "Emma? Emma?"

"I think the boy's arm may be broken, but they're okay!" Emma called back, looking at the young boy. She uncoupled his seatbelt for him and checked his legs. "I really think they're okay!"

Emma looked up, tears in her eyes. *Thank You, God,* she thought. *Thank You for letting them be okay.*

A cheer went up from the crowd down on the ice below the plane.

Suddenly the boy reached out his good arm and grabbed Emma's hand. "Bosco? Bosco! Where's my dog?"

"He's fine. He's outside," Emma said, and the boy relaxed.

"I can't believe it," the man said. "We could have frozen to death out here. Thank God you came."

"Thank God is right," Emma said fervently. "What happened?"

"We crashed," the boy said, and he gave a shy smile.

"Thank God for you," the man repeated, "and thank God for the fresh snow. That snow saved our lives."

"Are you sure you're okay?" Emma asked them again.

"We're fine," the man said, his voice getting brisk. "I can't believe that engine quit on me."

He looked around. "Where are we?"

"Long Lake near Route 7," Emma reported. "We're all staying at my aunt's house over there, and we saw your plane crash."

The man shook his head ruefully. "I can't believe we lived through that." He reached for his son and hugged him hard. "You sure you're okay?"

"Yeah, Dad, I'm fine," the boy said. "My arm hurts, but not too bad." He had big blue eyes and sandy-colored hair that fell over his forehead. He was very cute.

"We'll bring you back to our house," Emma promised him after she put his arm in a sling she found in the first-aid kit. "It's about a ten-minute walk or so from here. You're sure you can walk?"

"Can you, son?" he asked the boy.

"I'm okay, Dad," the boy insisted. "I'm not even bleeding or anything!"

"But both of you were knocked out," Emma reminded them. "You're going to feel a little unsteady."

"Well, first we have to get out of here," the man said. He got out of his seat and looked down from the open cockpit door at the people standing below.

"Need a hand?" Kurt called up to him.

"Two hands," the man said, and everyone laughed.

Gingerly the man climbed down from the plane, and then he, Kurt, and Billy lifted his son down. Finally Emma jumped down, too. As they set foot on the snow-covered ground, the brown dog danced up to them and practically knocked them to the ground with joy.

"Someone's happy to see you," Pres observed.

"We're happy to see him," the boy said, hugging the big dog. "Bosco! You're okay!"

"Bosco?" Becky repeated.

"He loves Bosco chocolate syrup," the boy said with a shy grin.

Becky smiled back at him.

"I'm Jim Magruder," the man, who looked to be about forty-five, said, "and this is my boy, Alex. I don't know how to thank you." He turned to Emma. "Especially you."

Emma blushed. "We couldn't have done this without each other."

"What happened?" Billy asked as the

166

group stood huddled around the wrecked plane.

"We were flying from Pittsfield, Massachusetts, up to Burlington," Mr. Magruder reported. "Our engine quit on us. Bad timing."

"Maybe we'd better talk about this at home," Sam suggested, her teeth chattering.

"Hey, at least you've got boots," Dee Dee said, looking down at her black suede shoes.

"Your feet must be freezing," Alex told her.

"Oh, well, it was worth it to save your life," Dee Dee told him. "I'm Dee Dee De Witt, by the way."

"Could you please flirt with him back at the house?" Sam asked archly.

"I was not flirting, for your information," Dee Dee retorted.

"Look, let's just move this show, okay?" Billy said.

"Good idea," Kurt said. "You up for a little walk?"

Mr. Magruder and Alex both nodded.

"It'll be a lot more fun than our last trip," Mr. Magruder said ruefully.

"So, Alex, tell me all about yourself," Dee Dee was saying as she walked beside Alex.

"God, she makes me sick," Allie told her sister.

"I heard that!" Dee Dee called to Allie.

"I don't care!" Allie called back.

"What do you say we take the lead so we don't have to listen to that?" Kurt suggested to Emma.

"I'm with you," Emma agreed.

Kurt led the way back to the house, Emma walking right next to him.

"I can hardly believe we saved them," Emma said softly.

"I'm so proud of you," Kurt said, taking Emma's gloved hand and giving it a squeeze.

"I'm so proud of *you*," Emma replied, her face beaming.

"Help!" came a voice from behind them. "Help!"

The whole group turned around.

Dee Dee was standing there, screaming and pointing at a hole in the ice.

Alex Magruder had somehow fallen through the ice and into the bone-chilling water of the lake.

He was thrashing around and calling for help as loudly as he could.

"Oh, God," Emma moaned.

"Help! Help!" Alex called. "Dad! Help!"

ELEVEN

"Must be a spring under there—weakened the ice," Kurt said grimly.

"Help!" Alex yelled again.

"What should I do?" Dee Dee cried. She held out her hand for him, reaching down.

"No, don't!" Kurt called quickly.

"But he's drowning!" Dee Dee sobbed.

"He'll pull you in!" Kurt yelled.

"But—"

"Help! Dad!"

"He won't pull *me* in. I'm heavier than he is," his father said, sliding across the ice to his son.

"Please, sir!" Kurt yelled. "I know what I'm talking about. It won't work!"

"I don't give a damn what you say!" Alex's dad said, reaching for his son.

"Wait, we can save him!" Kurt yelled. "Please!"

"Help me!" Alex yelled.

"Hold on, Alex!" Billy called to him.

"Don't panic!" Carrie told him. "You can float if you don't panic!"

"I'm freezing! Please, someone! Daddy!" Alex sobbed.

"We need to form a chain!" Kurt yelled. "Everyone, join hands. Stand as far away from the next person as you can. Hurry!"

Quickly everyone did as Kurt had suggested, their hands clasped tightly.

"Stretch out," Kurt called. "Stretch out as far as you can!" He slid toward the hole, where Alex was bobbing in the freezing water. "Keep going!" Kurt yelled. By the light of the full moon Emma could make out Sam and Pres at the end of the line.

"Okay!" Pres yelled.

"All right, everyone," Kurt called. "I'm going to reach in for Alex. Hold on tight.

On the count of three, tighten your grip and hang on for dear life. We're gonna pull him out!" Kurt leaned down to Alex. "We're gonna get you out, Alex, you hear me?"

"P-p-please hurry," Alex sobbed, his teeth chattering uncontrollably. "Please!"

Kurt grabbed Emma's wrist, and her hand tightened onto his wrist. Emma knew this was a stronger grip than just holding hands, and she reached for Alex's dad's wrist, explaining to him how to hold on and asking him to pass the information along.

Kurt said the ice might be thinner than we thought it was, Emma said to herself. *I hope it's strong enough to hold the rest of us!*

"One, two, three, hold tight!" Kurt yelled. He extended his free hand to Alex. "Come on, kid, you can do it!" Kurt urged him.

Alex reached up for Kurt, but bobbed away again before Kurt could grab him.

"Try again," Kurt said, his hand outstretched. He stood as close to the broken edge of the ice as he dared, and Emma held her breath. "Come on, Alex. Reach for me!"

Emma saw Alex's bare hand touch Kurt's gloved one, the fingers barely in his grasp. Kurt stretched his arm another few inches and wrapped his fingers around Alex's wrist.

"I can't hold on!" Alex screamed.

"You can!" Kurt insisted. "You can do it!"

Slowly, so slowly, with Emma straining behind him, Kurt managed to pull Alex toward him. His soaking-wet winter clothes made him a dead weight.

"Don't let go," Alex sobbed. Emma realized that the sharp, numbing cold must be taking a toll on the boy's ability to think. *We've got to get him out—now!*

"I won't let go," Kurt said. Emma felt his hand grip her wrist even more tightly as he struggled to pull Alex out. The human chain held fast, and finally Alex emerged from the deadly cold water.

"He's out!" Emma cried, tears streaming down her face.

Alex lay on the ice, sobbing.

His father ran to him and picked the boy up in his arms. "Alex!"

"Let's get him inside *fast*," Kurt said.

They all ran to the house, where they put Alex on the couch in the living room. He was very, very pale, and he was shaking uncontrollably.

Emma felt for his pulse. "It's very slow," she said in a low voice.

"Call a doctor!" Mr. Magruder begged.

"We can't," Sam told him. "The phone is out."

"Well, then, let's get him to the nearest hospital!"

"We can't do that either," Kurt said in a low voice. "The road is closed."

Mr. Magruder leaned over his son. "Alex? Alex, how are you doing?"

Alex's eyes were closed.

"Oh, God, we have to do something!" Mr. Magruder cried frantically.

"We've got to get his clothes off and get

him covered," Emma ordered, drawing on her knowledge of first aid. "Diana, Dee Dee, Becky, Allie—grab all the blankets you can find. Tina, Sam, Erin—go find my aunt's heating pad and hot-water bottle. Pres, put some more wood on the fire. Billy, Carrie, you go make some hot tea. Jake, Jay, Kurt—help me get these wet clothes off."

"Oh, God . . ." Mr. Magruder dropped his head in his hands.

Emma glanced at him. *A plane crash, and then his son falls through the ice . . . it's almost unbelievable that both of those things happened. No wonder he's panicking.*

Diana, Dee Dee, and the twins came back with a few blankets, and scurried off to get more while the boys pulled off Alex's wet clothing. Then they piled the blankets on top of him.

Emma felt for his pulse. "I think it's improving," she reported, checking the beats against the second hand of her watch. "But he's still got a ways to go. . . ."

Little by little they warmed Alex, with more blankets, an electric heating pad set on low, a hot-water bottle, and sips of hot tea. Through all of this activity, everyone worked smoothly with the others, speaking only in murmurs.

"He's up to a normal pulse!" Emma finally exclaimed.

"You're sure?" Mr. Magruder said, his voice shaking.

Alex opened his eyes, looked up at his father, and smiled faintly.

"There's your answer," Emma said softly.

Mr. Magruder hugged his son, tears of happiness running down his cheeks.

Emma looked around the room at her friends, Diana, Dee Dee, the twins, and Tina, who had all worked together to save the lives of two strangers. "Good job, guys," she said in a quiet but heartfelt voice.

Bosco barked his agreement.

Dashing through the snow
In a one-horse open sleigh

O'er the fields we go
Laughing all the way!
Bells on bobtails ring
Making spirits bright
What fun it is to laugh and sing
A sleighing song tonight!

"Hey, what's a bobtail?" Tina called out.

"Who knows?" Becky called back.

"Who cares?" Allie added.

Jingle bells, jingle bells, jingle all
the way
Oh what fun it is to ride in a
one-horse open sleigh!

It was the next evening, and everyone was in great spirits. Somehow the miracle of the night before had changed everything. And even though there was hardly any food, the house was incredibly overcrowded, and many of the people were strangers to each other, no one was fighting anymore.

Route 7 was still not open, although the radio reported that it would be the following morning.

Which meant that it was Christmas Eve, and they were all still stuck there. Together.

They cheerfully set out to prepare Christmas Eve dinner, which involved three cans of tuna fish; that amounted to about two bites of tuna per person. They popped the very last of the popcorn. Becky found a really old bag of marshmallows, which they roasted in the fireplace. Afterward they all sat in the living room in front of the fire, the Christmas tree shining with homemade decorations, and sang every single Christmas song they knew.

"Oh, who knows the one that starts, 'Chestnuts roasting on an open fire . . .'?" Tina asked eagerly. "I love that one!"

"Let Pres sing it," Billy suggested. "He sounds like a Southern Nat 'King' Cole!"

"Come on, big guy," Sam teased, tickling Pres in the ribs. "Let us all swoon over your voice."

Pres began to sing, softly strumming his guitar. He sang the song simply, sweetly. When he had finished you could hear a pin drop in the room.

"That was so wonderful," Tina said wistfully.

"It reminds me of home," Pres said. "Back in Tennessee, my whole family gets together for Christmas, and we sing all the old songs. . . ."

"Are you sorry you're not home?" Sam asked him.

He smiled at her. "No, sweet thang. Home is where the heart is, right?"

Sam grinned. "Dang, but you Southern boys are sweet talkers!"

Carrie sighed. "I wish we could at least call our families," she said wistfully, looking at the still-dead phone.

"I wish Dad were here," Becky said. "It's so weird, having Hanukkah without him."

"I wish Mom were here," Allie said.

No one said a word. For once neither Dee Dee nor Diana said something nasty.

"Hey, I have an idea!" Carrie cried impetuously. "I read it in a book once."

"What is it?" Billy asked her with a grin.

"Well, we all have wishes, right? And the holidays are just the time when wishes can come true—I really believe that!"

"My wishes already came true," Mr. Magruder said, smiling at his son.

"How about if we each write down our wishes and put them on the tree?" Carrie said.

"Kind of like wishing on a shooting star?" Allie asked.

"Right!" Carrie agreed. "They'll be our most secret, from-the-heart wishes, okay?"

"I'm in," Sam said. "But I can tell everyone what mine is—a decent meal."

Emma got paper from the desk in the corner, and she brought over a stack of pens, which she handed out to everyone. She handed paper and a pen to Kurt last.

"Hey," he said quietly, pulling Emma toward him.

"What?"

"What if my wish is you?"

Emma kissed him softly. "Then I'm very happy."

"Me too," he said. He took the paper and pen and began to write.

What is my most secret, heartfelt wish? Emma wondered. *What do I really want more than anything in the world?*

At that moment, Sam and Carrie were both having the exact same thought as Emma.

My life is so terrific, Carrie thought. *But there's so much I want . . . for Billy's father to be all better, for the Flirts to get their CD released, for me to get straight A's at Yale . . .*

Sam chewed pensively on the end of the pen. *What can I wish for?* she thought. *All I want is . . . well . . . everything! I want to be rich and famous. I want to have a zillion crazy adventures. . . .*

And so everyone sat there, thinking and then finally writing.

"This is so cool!" Tina cried as she folded her wish into a small square.

"Hey, how do we attach them to the tree?"

"Any way you want," Carrie said as she folded up her wish. "Under an ornament is good."

"Between the branches works," Sam said, placing her wish on the tree.

"Hey, who's up for a snowball fight?" Jake asked after everyone had put their wish on the tree.

"Whoever heard of a Christmas Eve snowball fight?" Erin asked huskily.

"Hey, so we'll start a new tradition!" Jake said.

"But we'll also burn up calories," Sam protested. "And then we'll be even hungrier!"

"Tomorrow morning, when the road opens, we'll all go eat the biggest breakfast in the history of breakfasts," Carrie said happily.

"God, you people are just so perky!" Sam groaned.

Pres started throwing pillows and cushions at her from the couch.

"Okay, okay, I'm in, I'm in!" Sam laughed. "I give up!"

"Maybe you'd better rest that arm, Alex," Mr. Magruder suggested.

"I guess so," Alex said, sounding disappointed.

"I'll keep him warm," Dee Dee promised.

Alex blushed red.

"Well, it looks like his circulation is fine," Diana teased him.

Everyone ran to change into warm clothes for the snowball fight, then they all tumbled down the stairs and out into the snow.

"Guys against the girls!" Jay cried out, leaning over to make a huge snowball.

"Hey, no fair, you guys throw too hard!" Dee Dee protested.

"Let's just make it a free-for-all," Billy said, forming a snowball. "Hey, Carrie, this has your name on it!" He heaved the snowball at Carrie, and it hit her smack in the stomach.

"I'll get you!" she yelled, quickly making a snowball and throwing it back at Billy. It caught him on the arm.

Soon everyone was making and throwing snowballs. Erin made a big one, which she heaved at Diana with all her might. It caught Diana unawares, knocking her over. She sat there in the snow, dumbfounded, as everyone gathered around her.

"Are you okay?" Erin rasped anxiously. "I didn't mean to hurt you."

"Nothing is bruised but my ego," Diana said with dignity. She lay back in the snow. "Ever make a snow angel?"

"I haven't done that in years!" Emma exclaimed. She lay down near Diana and spread her arms and legs wide, sweeping them back and forth through the snow. Then she jumped up. "A perfect angel!"

"Trust a girl who always wears white to make a perfect snow angel," Sam teased her. She fell over onto the soft snow. "Wow. Look at all the stars."

Everyone plopped down into the pillowy snow and stared up at the starry night.

"It's so beautiful," Tina sighed. "I wish I could stay here forever and ever."

"Was that your wish?" Emma asked her softly.

Tina didn't answer. The others got up to throw more snowballs, but Tina and Emma sat quietly together in the snow.

"You know that wish can't come true, don't you?" Emma said.

"Yeah," Tina admitted.

"Your parents must be really worried about you by now," Emma said.

"Yeah," Tina said again. She lay back down in the snow. "Why can't my life be like this, though? Peaceful and fun, with people who love each other?"

"We don't all love each other," Emma pointed out. "We're not even friends with Diana. And Becky and Allie aren't very fond of Dee Dee, either."

"But you and Kurt are totally in love," Tina said in a small voice. "And Pres loves Sam, and Billy and Carrie are crazy about each other. It must be so great. . . ."

"It is," Emma admitted. "But Kurt and

I have had our problems. Sometimes we still do."

"Really?" Tina asked.

"Really," Emma said. "Nothing is perfect. Not even when you love someone with your whole heart."

Tina was silent for a moment, staring up at the stars. "But what about you and Sam and Carrie?" the younger girl said. "You guys really love each other. I'd give anything in the world to have best friends like you guys."

"It will happen," Emma said.

"How do you know?" Tina asked plaintively.

"Because you're such a terrific person," Emma told her. "Terrific people end up with terrific friends."

"So how come I don't have any terrific friends now?" Tina asked.

"Maybe you've been too afraid to let people see who you really are," Emma said gently.

Tina was silent again. "I guess I really can't stay here forever, huh?"

"Right," Emma admitted.

"That's not what I wrote and put on the tree, anyway," Tina admitted. She looked up at the stars again. "I wrote that I wished my parents would get back together." She looked at Emma again, and there were tears in her eyes. "But I guess some wishes don't ever come true."

"I have an idea," Emma said. "Why don't we go back into the house? You can write another wish for the tree. Something for yourself. Something that you could make happen."

"Okay," Tina said shyly. "It's a good idea."

"We'll be right back, everybody!" Emma called out. The others were all happily shrieking and pelting each other with snowballs a few feet away.

Emma and Tina went into the house and walked into the living room. Alex had fallen asleep on the couch; Dee Dee was nowhere to be seen.

"Someone's wish fell off the tree," Tina said, going to pick it up. She handed it to Emma.

This wish had come unfolded. Emma

recognized Diana's handwriting. And before she could stop herself, she had read what Diana had written: "I wish I was back in the Flirts. I wish I had someone to love."

TWELVE

"... A single lane is now open on Route 7; however, travelers are advised to proceed with caution. ..."

"Hey, everyone, the road is finally open!" Carrie yelled. It was the next morning—Christmas Day. She was in the kitchen with Billy, listening to the radio as they prepared the very last of the food for Christmas breakfast. It consisted of half of a peanut butter sandwich per person, some crackers, some raisins, and an ancient can of mocha frosting.

Emma hurried into the kitchen. "Did I just hear you say the road is open?"

Carrie nodded and licked the peanut

butter off the knife. "They just said so on the radio."

At that moment Jay came racing into the kitchen as well. "Hey, the road is open!"

"We know," Billy said. "The radio was just talking about Route 7."

"No, no, I mean I saw a snowplow on the road that runs behind the house. Now all we have to do is shovel the cars out and open a path to the road."

Billy groaned good-naturedly. "That's gotta be a hundred and fifty yards!"

"The road's open? That means we don't have to eat *that* for breakfast!" Dee Dee said from the doorway.

"That means we can get a plane to Hawaii!" Diana added from behind Dee Dee.

"Since all of you extra guests are going to be out of here in a little while—" Emma began.

"And we're gonna get food!" Sam added. "Real food! Yes!"

"And real privacy," Pres added, pulling her close.

"I can't think about love right now," Sam protested. "I'm too hungry!"

"Let's go pack," Dee Dee told Diana. "We're out of here!"

"What I started to say before," Emma said before they left, "is that maybe we could open the presents before you all leave."

"You guys can open them after we're gone," Alex said.

"Right," his dad said. "We don't want to horn in on your celebration, now that we can leave."

"But there are presents for everyone," Tina said. "That's what Emma was trying to tell you!"

Diana folded her arms. "Surely she's kidding."

"No," Emma said. "She's not."

"But . . . we don't even celebrate Christmas," Allie said tentatively.

"Well, it's Hanukkah, too, isn't it?" Tina said. "You told me so yourself!"

"True," Becky agreed with a small smile. "But we don't have presents for anyone."

"Well, we do!" Tina cried. "They're from

me and Emma and Sam and Carrie, right?"

Sam, Emma, and Carrie smiled at Tina.

"Right," Carrie said warmly.

"So that's what you were doing last night when I was cold and lonely?" Billy teased Carrie.

"Come on," Tina urged. "Let's go into the living room!"

The whole group ran into the living room, and Sam, Emma, Carrie, and Tina began to bring boxes and bags out from behind the couch.

"This is incredible!" Erin exclaimed.

"I know!" Tina agreed happily. "It's so cool!"

"We figured all of us in the Flirts—and Kurt and Carrie—could open our presents to each other after everyone else is gone," Emma explained.

"I guess that leaves me out," Diana said, trying to sound as though she couldn't care less.

"So we thought that the rest of you could open your presents from us now," Carrie added.

"Becky and Allie, you first!" Tina cried, handing each girl a gift wrapped in old newspapers.

"Sam, it's your sweater!" Becky cried when she opened hers.

"Well, you already stole it from me," Sam said, trying to sound gruff. "I might as well just give it to you."

"And your Yale sweatshirt!" Allie said, grinning at Carrie. "This is so incredibly nice of you! I love it!"

"Now you, Mr. Magruder," Tina urged. She handed him a small package wrapped in aluminum foil.

"A book!" he said, turning it over so he could see the title. "*She's Come Undone*, by Wally Lamb." Everyone laughed together.

"It's not really about flying even though there's a flying leg on the cover," Tina told him, "but I saw it upstairs on the bookshelf, and Emma said her aunt wouldn't mind if we gave it to you."

"Thank you," Mr. Magruder said, grinning ear to ear. "I'll treasure it always!"

"Alex, this is for you," Tina said shyly,

handing the boy a flat present wrapped in a brown paper bag.

He opened it quickly. Inside was a beautiful drawing pad. "Wow," he breathed. "That's really nice."

"You told me you like to draw," Tina said. "I already used a couple of sheets of paper, but most of it is there."

"Thanks!" Alex said eagerly. "I'll draw something for you and send it to you, okay?"

"Okay," Tina said, her eyes shining with happiness.

"That means you have to give him— and us—your address," Kurt pointed out.

"Yeah, I guess it does," Tina agreed.

Everyone turned to look at Diana, the only person who wasn't in the Flirts who hadn't received a present.

"I guess you don't have anything for me," Diana said lightly. "Hey, that's okay. I don't care or anything."

"But we do have something for you," Tina insisted. She looked over at Dee Dee, who looked at Diana.

"I kind of helped them with this. I hope you don't mind," Dee Dee said.

"What are you talking about?" Diana asked.

Carrie unfolded a piece of notebook paper and propped it up in front of herself, Tina, Emma, and Sam. Then she picked up Pres's acoustic guitar. "This is a song by Diana De Witt—"

"Hey!" Diana protested. "Where did you get that? I threw it into the fire!"

"You had another copy in your notebook," Dee Dee said sheepishly. "I gave it to them. It has all the guitar chords with the lyrics and everything."

"This song is called 'The Wish,'" Carrie said in a firm voice. "I'm not much of a guitar player—Billy's been trying to teach me—but I'll do my best."

And then Carrie, Emma, Sam, and Tina sang Diana's song.

Some girls wish for money
And some girls wish for fame
Some girls wish for wishes, but that's
   just a silly game.

Some girls wish for diamonds
And some girls wish for pearls.
Some girls wish for everything they've
    ever seen or heard.

But when I make three wishes
Each wish is just the same
I wish I could let you see who I really
    am . . .
Oh yes, I wish I could let you see who
    I really am.

When the four girls finishing singing,
the room was very, very quiet. The only
sound was the crackling from the fireplace.

"I know it isn't very good," Diana finally said in a hard, cold voice.

"But it is," Billy said. "It's beautiful."

"Diana, it's real fine," Pres drawled.

"I . . . I . . . it's just a song, you
know," Diana said nervously. "I mean, it
isn't personal. It doesn't mean anything."

"Yes, it does," Tina said.

"Now how would you know?" Diana
said sharply.

"Because I'm just like you," Tina said earnestly. "I don't let people see who I really am, either, so I know exactly how it feels."

Diana turned away from the group, but not before Carrie saw a tear trickling down her face.

Well, who would have thought it? Carrie marveled. *This really is the season of miracles!*

"They're all gone. I can't believe it!" Emma said, throwing herself down on the couch.

"And I have a full stomach," Sam added with a contented sigh. "I'm a new woman."

"I never saw someone suck up so much of one breakfast buffet," Pres teased her.

It was that afternoon, and finally Dee Dee, Diana, Alex, Mr. Magruder, and Tina had all been dropped off in Burlington. The phone had even started working again; before they left, Tina had called her parents, Allie and Becky had called their dad, and everyone else had called their families to wish them a merry Christmas.

In Burlington, after they'd all eaten at a restaurant, Mr. Magruder had rented a car, and he had promised Emma he would drive Tina all the way home on his way back to Massachusetts and make sure she actually walked through her front door. He said it was the least he could do. Alex and Tina looked very happy to be going on a long car trip together. Bosco wagged his tail.

Diana and Dee Dee had been deposited at the airport to catch a flight to New York, where they could connect to a flight to Hawaii. Mr. Jacobs, who had been frantic with worry over the twins, picked the twins up at the restaurant. Becky and Allie hugged their dad as if they never wanted to let go.

The rest of them had stopped for some groceries, then returned to the cabin.

"I have to say, this was truly the most bizarre Christmas of my entire life," Carrie said as she lay down in front of the rekindled fire.

"I'll second that," Billy said, taking Carrie into his arms. "It may take me until New Year's Eve to recover!"

"That song of Diana's was kind of amazing, wasn't it?" Erin asked, her head on Jake's shoulder.

"No kidding," Jake agreed. "I guess there is actually a real person inside her!"

"So why does she work so hard at proving she's such an unfeeling witch?" Jay asked.

Emma shrugged. "She's scared, I guess."

"Oh, please," Sam groaned. "Don't anyone tell me I'm supposed to feel sorry for Diana. She's gorgeous, she's rich—"

"She's lonely," Carrie put in.

"So?" Sam asked. "That's her own fault. Hey, who's up for the hot tub?"

"Not me," Erin said. "I'm still fighting this cold, or whatever it is. I'm going to go lie down."

"And I think I'll lie down with her," Jake said innocently. They walked away, their arms around each other.

"Ah, young love. So sweet," Sam trilled. She got up from the couch and stretched. "Okay, I'm ready to get naked and wallow in hot water."

"Sounds good to me!" Pres agreed.

"On second thought, big guy," Sam said, "maybe this should be a girls-only kind of deal. Because you know the sight of my perfect body would drive you too wild to be able to control yourself."

Pres laughed and gave Sam a hug. "Did I tell you today how great you are?"

"Not today, no, I don't believe you did," Sam mused.

"Well, then, I'll tell you later," Pres decided. "When we're alone."

"It's a date," Sam quipped. "Okay, ladies, let's go get naked!"

"Bye, guys!" Emma said, giving Kurt a quick kiss.

"Don't leave me!" Billy told Carrie dramatically.

"I promise to give you the world's greatest back rub later tonight," Carrie told him, sealing it with a kiss.

"Why am I always the only one without a woman?" Jay moaned.

"We definitely have to find Jay a girlfriend!" Carrie said with a laugh.

"Hey, I just thought of something," Sam said. "We haven't even given each other our presents yet!"

"This afternoon," Billy said, "okay?"

"We'll be there!" Sam called as she, Emma, and Carrie headed out back to the hot tub.

They quickly stripped down and jumped into the steaming water.

"Oh, tell me this isn't bliss," Sam said, sinking back into the water.

"Heavenly," Emma murmured.

"Almost as heavenly as Billy," Carrie said, closing her eyes and leaning back, "but not quite."

For a long time the three girls were quiet, letting the tension of the last few days ease away.

"You know, I must be losing my mind," Sam finally said, "but I almost . . . *liked* the monsters this time."

"They're growing up," Carrie said.

"I really liked lighting that snow menorah," Sam said softly. She splashed her hand in the water. "Maybe I should learn more about Hanukkah and stuff. . . ."

"Ask Susan," Emma suggested. "I'm sure she'd send you a book."

"Yeah," Sam agreed. "You know, it's so bizarre. I love Christmas, I really do. It's my all-time favorite holiday. But I felt something really special when I lit that menorah."

"It really is okay, Sam," Carrie said. "You're special. You can love both."

"Yeah, I guess I can," Sam said thoughtfully. She closed her eyes again and let her hair swish around in the water. "I am so comfortable. I'm never getting out of here."

"Do you think things will work out for Tina?" Carrie asked.

"She's actually a wonderful girl," Emma said. "I think she'll be okay. Last night I suggested that she write a wish for the tree that was a wish she could actually make come true. And she told me what she wished for."

"What?" Carrie asked.

"Best friends like you," Emma said softly.

Carrie sat up in the water. "That's hilarious! Because that was my wish, too, in a way. I wished that the three of us would always be best friends."

"Me too!" Emma exclaimed.

"You're not going to believe this," Sam said, "but I did, too!"

They all stared at each other a moment, then broke out laughing.

"We really are lucky, aren't we?" Emma said, her eyes shining.

"Yeah," Carrie agreed. "We really are. Merry Christmas, you guys."

"Merry Christmas," Emma echoed.

"Happy Hanukkah!" Sam said with a laugh. "Happy everything! I love you guys!"

"May all our wishes always come true," Emma said softly.

"They will," Sam predicted. "Guys may come and go—"

"Not our guys!" Carrie protested.

"Maybe not," Sam said, "but no matter

205

what, best girlfriends are forever, know what I mean?"

No one needed to answer, because they all knew.

Love was the greatest miracle of all.

SUNSET ISLAND MAILBOX

Dear Readers,

Happy holidays to you! Whether you celebrate Christmas or Hanukkah or something else or nothing, I wish you happiness and all the luck in the world for the new year. Can you believe the turn of the century is just a few years away?

So, what'd you think of <u>Sunset Holiday</u>? So many readers had written me requesting a story where the gang gets snowed in together that I just had to write one for you! Which just goes to show that I still want this series to be everything you want it to be.

Many, many Sunset sisters have contacted me at America Online, which is very exciting! My e-mail address there is authorchik@aol.com, and it is really fun to get mail from you and sometimes even "chat" with you online. You'll find many of your Sunset sisters there—look for the "private room" called Authorchik in the "teenscene" area. I'm sometimes there, with Jeff, too!

Great stuff is happening with the fan club, too. I know that many of you have found new pen pals from the pen pal list, and I know that many of you also have been playing the Sunset Trivia game! Nothing makes me happier than when one Sunset sister finds another one to be her bud.

Now, on to something more serious. You know I get a lot of mail. I got the following from a Sunset sister who is a frequent correspondent and a friend. I wanted to reprint this letter for you—I've taken her name out to protect her privacy.

The really awful thing is that I've gotten several letters like it. From girls just like you, from all over the country. This is horrible. Girls to whom a terrible thing happens, but who don't want to tell their parents about it.

Please—don't keep silent. Don't let boys get away with a major crime. Don't be afraid to tell an adult. Because if a boy tries to rape you, or does rape you, if you let him get away with it, then he's really raped you twice.

Think about it.

See you on the island!
Best-
Cherie Bennett

Cherie Bennett
c/o General Licensing Company
24 West 25th Street
New York, New York 10010

All letters printed become property of the publisher.

Dear Cherie,

The whole time it happened she was telling herself it was not . . . and as his hands ran across her skin it sent a chill through her body and again she had to remind herself that this was not happening. And she sat there, crying at first, begging him to stop, crying out for help, and realizing that they would not help. And Tori Amos sang on from the radio, "This is not really happening . . ."

She felt the warm tears falling down her cheeks onto his shirt and she felt him shudder and let up a little and finally he released her and she got up as if nothing had ever happened and walked into the room to chat with the man she thought she loved who had sat there laughing as this all happened . . . as she had nearly been raped by her own boyfriend's bud.

And later that night she stood in the shower, her head against the cool tile and tried so hard to wash the dirty feeling from her body . . . why should she feel dirty if nothing had happened?

And the next day she felt almost successful about convincing herself that nothing had happened. She jokingly went up to her boyfriend and showed him the bruise left on her chest by the beating his best friend had given her . . . along with the numerous purple bruises on her neck and shoulders.

But a different guy friend did not find those bruises as funny as her boyfriend did . . . he called her aside and talked to her . . . and once again what happened came to life, and she felt her stomach retch.

She walked up to her best girlfriend and told her what happened and she gave her a hug and that is when the first tears fell. All period she sat there and shed bitter tears as her classmates looked at her with mixed looks of pity and sorrow and amusement and the worst looks . . . the looks of disbelief.

And she sits here now typing on her typewriter and she still feels numb, and she has these feelings of irony, and dirtiness, and she is waiting in silence for the curtain to fall so that she can go back to her normal life . . . clean and pure and happy . . . and also sane and carefree.

But she knows that her life will never be the same and it is that thought that makes her cry . . . it is that thought that causes the tears to fall down her girlish cheeks and onto her many bruises.

—*Name and address withheld*

CHERIE BENNETT
BELIEVERS
F A N   C L U B

Hey, Readers! You asked for it, you've got it!

Join your Sunset sisters from all over the world in the greatest fan club in the world...
Cherie Bennett Believers Fan Club!

Here's what you'll get:

★ a personally-autographed-to-you 8x10 glossy photograph of your favorite writer
   (I hope!).
★ a bio that answers all those <u>weird questions</u> you always wanted to know, like how
   Jeff and I met!
★ a three-times yearly newsletter, telling you <u>everything</u> that's going on in the worlds
   of your fave books, and me!
★ a personally-autographed-by-me membership card.
★ an awesome bumper sticker; a locker magnet or mini-notepad.
★ "Sunset Sister" pen pal information that can hook you up with readers all over the
   world! Guys, too!
★ and much, much more!

So I say to you – don't delay! Fill out the request form here, clip it, and send it to the
address below, and you'll be rushed fan club information and an enrollment form!

Yes! I'm a Cherie Bennett Believer! Cherie, send me information and an
enrollment form so I can join the **CHERIE BENNETT BELIEVERS FAN CLUB!**

My Name _____

Address _____

Town _____

State/Province _____ Zip _____

Country _____

CHERIE BENNETT BELIEVERS FAN CLUB
P.O. Box 150326
Nashville, Tennessee 37215 USA

Items offered may be changed without notice